DEARLY BE*LOVED*
S.I.S.T.A.S

A Novel By:
Liltera R. Williams

Liltera R. Williams

Dearly Beloved S.I.S.T.A.S

iWrite4orU Publishing
Website: www.iwrite4oru.com
Email: contact@iwrite4oru.com

Editor: Sharon Denny

Cover Image Courtesy of iStockPhoto

Cover Arranged by: Riana Winters

ISBN: 978-0-615-82130-6

Printed in the United States of America

Liltera R. Williams

Table of Contents

Part I

Part II

Part III

For the woman who has lost her faith... There's hope...

Part I

Liltera R. Williams

"For God has not given us a spirit of fear, but of power and of love and of a sound mind"

– 2 Timothy 1:7

Liltera R. Williams

Sheila

Liltera R. Williams

Chapter 1:
Something That Starts with an S

If the ray of light offers an ounce of hope, I am seeking to find it in all the wrong places. The seasons of spring and summer trump fall and winter with grace, and I am longing for infinite moments of watching the sun rise and set over a shadowlike horizon. Sunshine is a sacred sin, and darkness scares me. My name is Sheila, but you can call me Sunni … with an *I*. I tend to be brighter when I am her. Even when I attempt to say what I mean and mean what I say, no one comprehends my story.

I wish my sistas were here. I've secluded myself from them while searching for something — something that starts with an *S*. But *S* words hardly ever suited me to the point of offering the benefit of safety. I desire to be set free. My husband, Carl, just doesn't love me enough to let me soar. He actually doesn't even know that my self-consciousness relies heavily on his ability to be selfish. I need him to not need me because lately I have been overtaken by the serenity of peace, and my sexuality has always been a secret. I'm not too full of shame to admit that sometimes I cry for comfort. I just can't seem to receive it from someone who is in sync with my cravings for acceptance. Carl is a man — a man whom I love, but he is not my soul mate. And I think Sunni is beginning to wish I didn't exist. I have somehow allowed fear to steal my joy, and she's probably too busy to even see it. I also may be too shy to approach her with an honest statement that bears all truth. Truth has never been my strongest offering. This is why I must study her from a distance. I refuse to allow her to examine the scars that were sculpted by him. I cannot freely share the details of the turmoil he has caused, mostly because they are always watching, and I don't want them to know how stupid I once was. Even if I was able to develop a clear understanding of it all, she would not get me. I don't know where this shadow of a life is taking me, but it feels like the walls are shifting in. These sounds of blackness are too silent for me to absorb like the soft sponge that I am. Who can I call on to rescue me from slumber? I sleep my days away and damage my skin with pointy tools that cause me to bleed a salty red substance. It seems to be my favorite color lately. I try to invent flashbacks from memory, but I can only remember the blow from Carl's last punch. It struck me so hard.

As I was drifting on a memory, trying to reminisce over a time when love wasn't so sickening, I could only recall the moment right before I ended up here in this sanitized vault. It's easy to ignore salacious urges when savageness does not stimulate your mind, or your vagina. Frequently suffused by misfortune, it's no wonder I am currently in a snake pit six feet under, right above hell. Bitterness has engulfed me, and I am swimming in a pool, stroking my way to becoming a stonewashed remnant of yesterday's shame. If this is how it feels to die alone, stoic and slavishly defiled, I would rather live to dodge bullets and fists until I am able to singlehandedly rule the world with my subsistent and impulsive strategies. But in a restless, supine position, I am only allowed to submit to torture at the hands of my husband, and my therapist keeps telling me that my past is to blame. Domestic violence isn't classified as a true crime, no matter the severity of the assault. Reporting his reoccurring manhood violation would be both inconvenient and pointless. So, I tell them that I harmed myself. Besides, they already think I'm crazy.

At the prime of her life and with nowhere else to turn, Sheila had already experienced more than she could bear. She knew this was her breaking point. It was always difficult for her to prosper after many years of corruption, which led to animosity and full-blown disdain. There wasn't much to cleave to from her childhood; every memory had vacated from her mind, with no consent to return, and that's how she preferred it. Sheila could never forget her sistas, though. They would forever be a part of her. Their kinship was an endless obligation for sure — an affiliation that no one could perceive clearly. How could Sheila explain what she has been going through for the past seven years? To them, she had it all. But the things that were happening in the dark kept forcing their way to the light, and Sheila could not tame her newfound love, Sunni. She was her own woman.

"What if she's in cahoots with Brenda?" Sheila thought.

She never really planned to allow her past and present to coincide. Sunni wasn't one of Sheila's sistas; she was her partner. She wanted Faith to know Sunni … to love her just as much. Brenda would just nag her away and she couldn't lose that necessary connection. Although it's been a while since they'd all enjoyed time together in one common space, Sheila missed having them there. She thought it meant that she was getting better, but then Sunni showed up and Carl turned vicious. For two years, she was able to think clearly and in advance. Work was going well and her marriage hadn't reached this crucial point yet. She created a whole new life and was living it without any interruptions. Then, she found out that she was pregnant. Sheila never really wanted children. She couldn't handle the pressure of being responsible for another life and Carl knew it, too. They discussed the possibilities, but Sheila was afraid—too afraid of running out of lifelines. She couldn't even save herself. An infant would not stand a chance with her genetics. So, she had an abortion; it was the second time. Carl didn't know anything about the first one, but when baby number three was announced, he tried to force her to make another inhumane decision. Sheila wondered how it was so easy for her to end two lives that were previously growing inside of her. Although she suffered through a great load of remorse and distress, that's how it's always been. She made mistakes and dealt with them until they were forgotten. Her memory wasn't always reliable. Sheila knew that she would eventually be sequestered from anything that resembled normal. That was clear as soon as she became a teenager. Her dysfunctional upbringing fueled the predicaments of her future and she didn't want her daughter to be condemned by the effects of a disorder that she couldn't regulate. Over time, she believed that she would somehow find herself—her real self. She just didn't know exactly when. Living in the unknown made Sheila feel like she wasn't actually living ... just existing. She could be defined by her social security number, but not by her personality. It was interchangeable. Conversations with her sistas left her in a discombobulated state more often than not. She needed clarity—to understand what was happening to her and why. Why did God make her suffer through so much? She started over, but no matter how hard she tried, she couldn't completely delete the old. And the new was getting harder and harder for her to seize. There was no one who truly understood her conflict — to wake up each day and not know how to proceed, because yesterdays keep evaporating and tomorrows are never affirmed. Carl's behavior could not be justified, but it was understood. Sheila knew why he flipped out every time she swapped back and forth. He wanted her to be a typical woman—a woman that would never change. Instead, she insisted on rearranging her appearance and frolicking to and fro with her sistas. The aftereffects were just never considered.

Sheila left home as soon as she turned eighteen, and somehow eased her way into college, but flunked out during her senior year. She didn't take time to actualize the pros and cons of moving back home. Her mother's latest plea for her to return kept replaying over and over again, but Sheila's mind was already made up. She wanted to be free and she wanted to disregard all previous occurrences that ever made her feel unworthy. Everything was so easy to forget, but when it was time to remember, her past was such a confusing blur.

Brenda

Liltera R. Williams

Chapter 2:
Shut Up!

It happened over twenty years ago, but it seems like just yesterday. Dr. Sebastian says it's normal for me to still be affected by it after so long. For the past few years I've been confessing my deepest secrets to her … once a week, every Tuesday … ever since my mama signed me up to be fixed. I didn't want to, but Faith begged me to go. She told me God can't save me unless I try to save myself. I just want to be free.

Dr. Sebastian usually knows what she's talking about. Today, I just don't feel like hearing what she has to say. "How are you feeling today, Brenda?"

I squirmed around on the couch, trying to get comfortable. She already knows how I'm feeling. Why does she have to ask?

"I'm fine, I guess."

"What does fine mean?"

"Fine means fine!" I tend to snap at her when she poses questions I already know she knows the answer to. Obviously, I'm not fine if I'm still making appointments with her, hoping she will share her sentiments and stop trying to be so damn professional all the time. I need a friend, not a chaperone.

"Well, it sounds like somebody is having a bad day. You want to tell me about it?"

"Not really."

"Talking about it will make you feel a lot better." That was her way of assuring me.

"I don't know where to start."

"Just start from the beginning like you always do. Your memory seems to be getting much better. Or you can start by telling me why you broke your mirror this morning. I'm ready to listen when you're ready to speak."

"I don't know. I just got tired of looking in it and seeing the same thing."

"What do you see?"

"A face that I don't recognize without my makeup."

"What do you suppose that means?"

"I don't know. You tell me."

"Well, I think you've hidden behind your makeup for so long that you're not accustomed to seeing what you look like without it. I think that's what's causing you not to accept who you really are."

"I guess looks can really be deceiving,"

"Brenda, people lie, mirrors don't. Sometimes it's just too hard to face the truth."

So much has been on my mind lately. I've been waiting all week to tell her about the things that have unfolded. I don't know if she's tired of hearing my story, but I know that it's helping her figure me out.

"Daddy's little girl? Not me. Well, not anymore. There are so many things that come along with fulfilling that title and I have failed to live up to those standards, only because my daddy has become the kind of daddy that you shouldn't look up to. I'm no longer a little girl. I've evolved into a woman and as I continue to travel the path that leads to womanhood I will keep losing pieces of my younger self, which scares me. Change is difficult, especially when you're becoming someone you don't want to be. I've lived almost my entire life trying to disassociate myself from the norm, but it's a struggle trying to find a way to be unlike others. I strive hard to be different because I don't want to do things that people expect, but mostly because I don't want to be exactly like him. If my mama would have never chosen to stay with my daddy, my life wouldn't be so fucked up. She knew he was no good, but she still stayed. They took everything from me."

"Everything like what, Brenda?"

"Everything. My whole fucking life has been controlled by superstition since I was swept away from that shithole. What kind of man takes advantage of his own daughter? It's been years and I still haven't forgiven him. Probably never will. I can't believe my mama married that scumbag. I don't have any other family and no man is going to ever truly love a sloven woman. No matter how confident I look or how beautiful I am, no one knows how I feel on the inside. I know how to hide pain better than anybody, but it's killing me. Some days I feel like I'm not going to make it. I've been dealing with this shit forever and I still can't escape the strife that seems to follow me around everywhere I go. I'm a scapegoat for stigmas and stints, trying to snuggle my way out of a safari of lies. How's that for a summation, Doc?"

"You're using lots of *S* words again."

"And?"

"Brenda, that means you haven't improved. It means you are still unaware of how deeply your past has affected you. It means you could have a medical condition that even I am unable to diagnose. And finally, Brenda, it means that you are not fine."

Dr. Sebastian said what she had to say and then she just kept writing — filling up blank sheets of paper with my confessions and documenting things that I wish I couldn't remember … just like Sheila does. I don't usually talk this much, so I guess she's surprised because she always has to ask questions to get it out of me. I stretched my legs out on the couch and stared up at the ceiling. Dr. Sebastian finally stopped writing and asked, "How has your drinking been? Are you still spending your evenings in bars?"

"Yes." I couldn't lie. I know I have a drinking problem, but it's the only thing that helps me escape the memories.

"I'm an alcoholic and a murderer. How am I supposed to live with that?"

"A murderer?"

Dr. Sebastian looked at me confused. I couldn't remember if I had told her the whole truth about that night.

"Who did you murder, Brenda?"

"I didn't tell you?"

"No, Brenda, you didn't."

"My daddy."

"Are you sure?"

"Not completely. I just keep seeing it in my dreams."

"Seeing what exactly?"

"A knife in his side and blood on my hands."

"Is anyone else in the dream, Brenda?"

"Yes, my mama."

"And what is she doing?"

"Yelling at me."

"Can you remember what she's saying?"

"What she was always saying. Calling me a slut and blaming me for her shortcomings."

"How did that make you feel, Brenda?"

"I can't explain it."
"Can you use an *S* word to describe it?"
"Shitty."

As far as Brenda was concerned, therapy was a waste of time. It's been over a decade and she still isn't cured. The medication surely never helped. All it did was made her tired and she couldn't drink alcohol while taking the sedation pills. They were supposed to help her forget, but she couldn't. Every piece of a detail kept connecting with another and when she put them all together, the picture was always the same. Many memories have been extracted from her mind, but she could recall some of the events clearly.

I'll never know what it means to be Daddy's sweet princess or Mama's silhouette. Daddy turned me sour and I could never follow in Mama's footsteps. The man who was appointed to protect me harmed me in the worst way possible. Mama could have stopped it, but she let him. She was never strong enough to move on after Daddy left her stranded. We never had family dinners. Daddy never took me to the park. Mama never said she was sorry. How am I supposed to act normal when this is all her fault? I am who I am because of her. Daddy fucked me multiple times and then left us. Mama blamed me because he left. I was a good daughter and she was a scorned wife. She never even tried to protect me. Instead, she kept calling me a slut. Like I was the one doing something wrong. I was well-known around the house as the little bitch that could. I could do everything that Mama refused to do and Daddy was paying close attention. I only wanted to be his perfect little girl. I wanted him to love me because Mama never did.

Daddy told me he loved me, but when he stripped my childhood away from me I stopped believing in the saying. Mama was too busy settling for his stale commitment, so she shushed me every time I tried to tell her. Now she thinks my sexuality is a phase, as if I'm some type of mislead student who doesn't have the ability to make straight *A's* even when the answers are staring me right in the face. There is nothing wrong with me. I was born this way, and I've always been me at all times. They just want to find a way to define it so that they can box me in the surplus with all the others. Common sense ain't so common. I'm glad God blessed me with it, even in the midst of this storm. I have to get out. I have to go. But where? Every time I try to escape, I end up right where I started. I need Faith to lead me, but

Mama stashed Faith away with all my other hopes and dreams. It's impossible to remain optimistic when your whole damn support system fails to lift you up. I needed to be protected. I needed to be acknowledged. And I needed my mama to believe that I was the prey and Daddy was the villain. But time goes on and I am who I am because of it. I like having sex with men and I'm nurturing an attraction to a woman that I recently met. So what if I've lost count of how many people I've slept with. It's my body and my prerogative. Now she suddenly wants to be my mama and look out for me. Well, she missed her opportunity. It's too late for that shit. Some men are too stubborn to say sorry and too sorry to stay put. Some mamas are, too. I will not forgive her that easily.

Mama was rarely ever home; she let her job consume her. I guess saving a stranger's life was more important to her than ever being involved in mine. When she was home, all they did was argue. The smallest thing would spark quarrels that never seemed to end.

"Get your shit out the middle of the floor," Mama yelled after tripping over the pile of stuff that included Daddy's toolbox and filthy boots.

"Your ass just needs to watch where you're walking at," Daddy replied.

"I'm so sick of your shit! I bust my ass at work all day and I have to come home and deal with this. The least you can do is clean up around here."

"Men ain't supposed to clean. How many times I gotta tell you that?"

"Since when do you consider yourself a man?"

Mama shouldn't have asked him that question. She was finally trying to stand up for herself and although it slipped out under her breath, she knew him well enough to know it would make him angry. He heard it. And he was angry. Again. Daddy rose to approach Mama and I saw the fear all over her face, preparing to be provoked. He gripped the corners of her chin with his left hand and offered her a threat, "Question my manhood again and I'll kill you. Understood?" Mama held back her tears as she answered, "Loud and clear." She didn't know I was standing in the hallway watching.

"Brenda!"

She was shouting my name and I pretended not to hear her.

"Brenda, get your ass out here and wash these dishes."

I slowly made my way to the kitchen. Daddy glanced over and winked at me as he addressed Mama's demand.

"Why don't you wash them, Debra? My daughter ain't no slave."

"She's my daughter, too, and she's going to do whatever I tell her to do."

"You still talking back to me?" Daddy knew she would bow down. So did I.

"No."

"That's what I thought."

I obediently followed Mama's orders and began to scrub a small plate with an intense force, similar to the way I scrubbed away the kiss Daddy overpowered me with right before Mama walked through the door that night.

"Shhh…I'm not going to hurt you, baby," he promised.

That was a lie. He always lied. But I believed him because he was my daddy and daddies are supposed to treat their little girls like royalty, but instead he treated me like a booty call. I thought I was important. I thought I mattered.

Every time Daddy touched me, it felt like I was going to die. I flat lined and revived myself from about twenty deaths before that bastard disappeared. I was always relieved when Mama finally came home. She usually arrived in the nick of time, but seconds too late for her to see what he was actually doing to me, and this time she was running behind again. She must have stopped somewhere because it never took her this long to arrive after he was done. I timed it perfectly. I knew Daddy would see me walking into the bathroom with my towel and I wanted her to catch him in the act. I wanted her to finally see that I am not a liar and that Daddy was a poor excuse for a man. I hopped in the shower and waited. After cleansing my body and rinsing away the suds, I pulled back the shower curtain to find Daddy standing there staring at my fully developed body. Puberty suddenly became my worst enemy. He was naked. I was so caught off guard that I couldn't bring myself to speak. I reached to grab a towel off the rack to cover up my parts that were no longer private. Then, Daddy began to walk toward me. He got close enough to reach out and gently caress the side of my face with the back of his hand. I jerked a bit, not knowing what he would do next. I backed away from his touch and ended up against the wall. He joined me in the bathtub.

"You're so beautiful," he said.

His breath smelled like a mixture of beer and onions. He leaned in to kiss me and I turned my head to the side, presenting him with my cheek. I lifted my left hand to wipe off the gesture and he used that opportunity to remove the towel. His hands roamed all over my body, finally settling on my butt and he ignored my pleas for him to stop. I knew I wasn't strong enough to fight back, so I screamed. He clamped his hand over my mouth and immediately quieted me. Then he turned the water back on and bombarded me while I was in the shower; he forced his way in and started to rub on my titties. I tried to get away, but he grabbed me and pushed me onto the bathroom floor. The cold tile stung my back and I tried to scream again, but his tongue blocked my effort. I let out a painful sigh and started crying as he slipped his oversized penis inside of me, like a sniper with careful aim. My body went numb. I counted to a hundred a thousand times until it was over. When he was done, he removed himself, kissed me on my forehead, whispered "I love you" in my ear, and left me in the bathroom to resume my shower. I hated it. I hated him. And I hated Mama for being late on purpose. With tears rolling down my face, I stumbled to my room, locked the door, and picked up the phone to call her. She didn't answer. I screamed at the top of my lungs because God didn't save me this time like Faith said He would. My world faded to black as I closed my eyes and desperately hoped that I would forget all about this terrible nightmare tomorrow.

Things weren't always this way. Mama and Daddy used to get along. He wasn't always so angry and she wasn't always so spiteful. I'm sure they loved each other even more before I was born. I probably messed everything up. Mama always told me that I was a mistake. I wasn't planned, but Daddy wanted her to have me. Now I know why I guess, but I didn't ask to be born. On my fifth birthday, Daddy bought me my first bicycle and taught me how to ride it. It wasn't long before I was balancing myself without the training wheels. That's what it feels like now—I'm on the ride of my life, but there is absolutely no balance. If I fall, he won't be there to catch me. Mama won't be either. I had a normal childhood, until Daddy started drinking. Mama drove him to it. He would rather spend his evenings gulping down cans of beer instead of being the head of the household and leading his family like he was supposed to. Mama made him feel weak. He never said so, but I could tell. I caught him crying once, but I never said anything. I wanted to comfort him through whatever he was dealing with. I just didn't know that it would lead to this.

Brenda woke up to the echo of her mother's voice. She was shocked by the amount of blood on her hands.

"Brenda, what the hell happened?" her mother inquired.

She was too afraid to speak.

"Tell me now, dammit!" her mother shouted. "Now!" in a tone filled with more anger and an inch of concern.

Her voice drew Brenda out of her spell.

"Daddy…" she paused.

"Daddy what?"

"Daddy raped me…" It took all the strength Brenda had to say it. She was afraid of her mother's response, but even more afraid of what would happen if the blood on her hands meant that her father was dead.

"What have I told you about lying, Brenda?" Her mother was not immediately swayed by her confession.

"I'm not lying, Mama. I swear he did!"

"That is enough! I don't want to hear any more of your lies! Go clean yourself up and help me get dinner started. Your Daddy will probably be back soon."

Daddy never came back and Mama never forgave me. All I remember is stabbing him in the side, and then he was gone. The motherfucker just dropped off the face of the earth, and Mama waited for his ass for years like a goddamn fool. Pathetic. I'll never be as desperate as her. I have too many options to choose from and there's no way that I will ever let a man control me … whether he's dead or alive. Any man who tries to control a woman doesn't deserve to carry on breathing. Daddies included. He's the reason why I still have trouble sleeping. Although my insomnia saves me from recalling the moments of his incestuous takeovers, I have not totally forgotten. Some stories are just too hard to make up and I knew Mama would find a way to flip it on me.

Brenda and Sheila have a lot in common, even though neither of them will admit it. Stubbornness is at the core of their contempt for proper etiquette, which is probably why it was so hard for Brenda to talk about her case that was never picked up by the courts. The public attorney told her mother that it would not be viewed as statutory rape if it wasn't reported the first time it happened and there were no apparent signs of child abuse to verify that Brenda fought back. The attorney insinuated that Brenda could have aroused her own father and maybe he ran away because he couldn't resist her and he felt ashamed. He also said that the authorities couldn't locate her father to even charge him with the crime. Case closed.

Brenda blamed her mother and then she blamed herself. The first time it happened, she was too afraid to tell anyone. The last time it happened, she told her mother and then she told Faith.

"I tried to tell Mama, Faith. I tried, but she wouldn't believe me!"

"You have to make her believe you, Brenda. Tell her to take you to the doctor. They can prove it."

"I can't."

"Why can't you?"

"Because."

"Because what, Brenda?"

"I just can't. Leave it alone, please."

"No, Brenda. I will not just leave it alone."

"Your daddy should pay for what he did to you."

"It doesn't matter if they can't find him."

"Don't worry, Brenda. God will handle it."

"I hope so. What if I go to the doctor and they tell me that something is wrong?"

"Something like what?"

"I don't know. I've just been feeling really weird lately. Not like myself."

"What do you mean?"

"I think I could be sick or something."

"Well, there's only one way to find out."

"Yeah. I guess so."

"You'll be fine, Brenda. Just tell your mama to get you checked."

"OK. I will. Thanks, Faith."

Brenda grew accustomed to the affection she often received from her father. She couldn't fight him and her mother couldn't stop it, even though she never even tried. The doctor's visit actually proved that Brenda was having her father's baby. Six weeks along. She would be a mother and a sister at the same time. The doctor asked her mother if she would allow Brenda to keep the baby. At thirteen, Brenda was only a baby herself. "Because she's a minor, we will allow you to make the final decision," the doctor said before leaving them alone to talk in private. As soon as the door slammed shut, Brenda's mother stood to face her. Brenda was sitting on the exam table covered in a blue medical gown, wearing nothing underneath, and still shaking from the news.

"Lift your gown up."

"What?"

"Just lift the damn gown up, Brenda."

Brenda lifted her gown and exposed her breasts. She was already a C-cup. Her mother was staring. Brenda wasn't sure what she was looking at exactly.

"What are you doing, Mama?" she asked.

She didn't respond verbally. Instead, she reached out her hand to rub Brenda's belly. Her tears were awakened by the circular motion.

"We can't keep it," she mumbled.

"Why, Mama?"

"Because every day he or she will remind me of what your father did to you and I can't deal with that."

"So you want to kill my baby?"

"It's not a baby, Brenda. It's a monster."

"Don't say that!"

"Calm down. You will understand this decision when you're much older. This is normal. I'm calling the doctor back in. Is there anything else you'd like to say before I do so?"

"I hate you!"

"I know."

Brenda told Faith more about the foreign relationship that developed with her father and Faith told her that she needed to pray and seek help. Her mother felt the same and wanted to help Brenda get over this traumatic period, so she signed her up for therapy. Brenda rarely thinks about the baby her mother made her slay; however, it was the first event in a long line of catastrophes that could potentially lead to her demise.

She needs help. That seems to be the general consensus amongst people who think they have the slightest idea of what I've been through. I can't live my life for others. I'm a secular believer — not an atheist, just a realist. Everyone else has conformed to religious practices, trying to prove themselves to some supernatural being that has yet to show his face. Where are you, God? Is my profane demeanor too mannish for you to correct? Am I not worthy to be saved? It's all just a bunch of bullshit. All of it. And I'm too fucking impatient to deal with anymore of anybody else's lies. From now on, I'm doin' me and I don't give a fuck what anyone has to say about it. They can all go straight to hell — Mama, Daddy, Faith, Sheila and whoever the fuck she keeps talking to when she thinks I'm not paying attention!

Liltera R. Williams

Sunni

Liltera R. Williams

Chapter 3:
Sunshine, Blue Skies

Every Monday, I follow her as she struts for miles, high heels clanging against the pavement and skirt constantly rising up her thighs. Long, flowing, pressed hair, espresso skin and strategically polished finger nails. Red is her favorite color. She hardly ever looks up to notice me. Sometimes she's way too busy to care or even be interested in how much I admire her or how much I'd kill for her to be all mine. I'm trying to rescue her from the man who has pierced her heart through its fragile center. If she allows me to fully show her how she's supposed to be loved, we'd exemplify beauty together. My confidence and power mixed with her intelligence and creativity — a match made in womanhood. My goal is not to sweep her off her feet. I am solely focused on showing her the true meaning of love. He obviously could care less about her sanity. It's my job to be the security guard and the surgeon, simultaneously. Since I can't get there in time before he beats her, I can only sew up her wounds with an act of sympathy.

No matter how many times I tell her she deserves better, the decision will always be hers. I'm not the controlling type. I refuse to persuade her to spend more time with me when she would rather be with him. Besides, I like being alone. It allows me more time to think about who I am and what I want. No man will ever love me more than I love myself. I wish Sheila was that smart. Instead, she tries to hide me every time she gets a chance, but Carl seems to have caught on to her diversion. He's beginning to love me more and I guess she's jealous. It's not my fault that he recognizes the differences between her and me. I hate having to step down when he's around. Sheila should know better. I can't teach her everything, though. You have to keep some secrets to yourself, but now I'm tired of playing along. I never really understood the phrase *coming out of the closet* anyway. Even though I've been enclosed for a short amount of time, I'm quickly running out of space for new, imaginary expeditions. I can't keep shoving all of these unnecessary items into the corners of my fears. They won't fit. Someday I'll be free from the humiliation and disappointment. I'll shed this uncomfortable disguise and make sure that everyone knows love has no preference. Sheila keeps failing to realize that I'm a strong Black woman. She wants me to hide, and I'm tired of pretending … tired of doing what she wants me to do. I'm tired of acting like somebody I'm not, tired of believing there's something wrong with me and tired of praying for God to fix it. I need something, or someone, to save me.

Sunni. Sweet sweet, Sunni. Sheila's good side — the alter ego she brought to life when Brenda became dormant and while Faith was obscure. She wondered if her sistas really cared for her. If they could deal with her as is. Sheila wanted to change, but she was now the prototype for an all-in-one persona — a nemesis to her own resilience, trying to spearhead a solo movement. And Sunni made her feel like she could do anything.

"I believe in you, Sheila."

"Really, Sunni?"

"Yes."

"Tell me why."

"I just do. You've overcome so much and I want to see you bloom."

"Wherever I go, will you come with me?"

"As long as I am welcome, I will be there."

Sunni hoped that she could keep that promise. She knew how much Sheila hated empty guarantees. Carl already had her indulged in enough deception. Sunni was Sheila's best friend and she was also hers. Sheila told her about how her other two sistas turned against her—how Brenda's malice made her feel guilty and how the pressure from Faith made her feel incapable of bringing honor to anyone that she was linked to. Still, she wanted to reconcile and have all of them living together as one big, happy unit. Sheila never got a chance to experience that type of cohesiveness. Sunni planned to acquaint her with more than she could ever fathom, but she had to figure out how to knock Carl out of the picture. He did not complement the frame. Yet, Sheila loved him, for reasons unknown. It was hard for Sunni to assert herself as a key player. She, too, was afraid of getting hurt and afraid that Sheila would emotionally suck her dry and not think twice about offering an even exchange for her philanthropic trials. Of course one should give without expecting anything in return, but Sunni wanted Sheila entirely—to the fullest extent of her femininity. She needed her to discern the notion of being unyielding. However, Sheila was incompetent when it came to recognizing who was for her and who was against her.

Liltera R. Williams

Faith

Liltera R. Williams

Chapter 4:
So Long Sucker

When a man loves a woman he isn't supposed to leave. Every day I wonder why he doesn't care enough to stick around—to fight for me instead of against me. I'm a good wife. A good friend. A good lover. A good Christian. I prayed hard for a man who would love me and treat me like a queen. When God answered my prayers and blessed me with a husband I just knew it was meant to be, but I guess I was wrong. Today, Savannah asked me why her daddy is hardly ever here. I didn't want her to lose any respect for the man she loves the most, so my response was simply, "I guess we don't make him happy." It's the truth. I can no longer appease his desire for fun because his type of fun is a direct opposition to my Christian views and beliefs. He suddenly changed on me. He stopped going to church, stopped saying I love you and he finally just stopped coming home. I will not disobey my Heavenly Father for an insecure sucker who cannot overcome his lustful demons. So, I guess he found someone else who was willing to satisfy his so-called needs. I couldn't believe the blatant disrespect when he urged me to join him at the strip club. Then two weeks later, he had the nerve to ask me to participate in a threesome with a total stranger — some woman named Sunni. I couldn't take it anymore. God told me to release and repent, so I did. The last thing he said to me was, "If you love me you will do whatever it takes to make me happy." I should have reiterated the true meaning of love in that last instance of scandalous disappointment and offense, but instead, my final words were, "Goodbye and God bless." In Corinthians 13 verses four through eight, the bible says, "Love is patient, love is kind. It does not envy, it does not boast, it is not proud. It does not dishonor others, it is not self-seeking, it is not easily angered, it keeps no record of wrongs. Love does not delight in evil but rejoices with the truth. It always protects, always trusts, always hopes, always perseveres. Love never fails." When love is one-dimensional, there's no bulls eye in sight. You'll always be aiming at an empty target if you're the only one trying to make it work.

Men won't continue to fight if they're winning somewhere else. So why should I keep throwing punches that don't even land anywhere near the target? Women have to be strong enough to just let go and let God. I've cried my last tear and I refuse to question God's scheduled plan for my life. I'm fully aware that He's in control, and as long as He's in my corner, I'll never stop believing in love. Prayer changes things, and I pray that Savannah grows to understand that she doesn't have to depend on a man to be happy. My husband is just going to have to pray for himself from now on.

Faith had had enough. Unlike Sheila, she was ready to let go of her husband and ready to leave it all in God's hands. She prayed for reconciliation, but it must not have been what she needed. Faith was always a firm believer that everything happens for a reason. Although she didn't understand why certain things happened, she never questioned God. Faith's calling was clear. She was a walking testimony, which is why her sistas depended on her so much. No matter what Faith was forced to deal with, she always followed God's lead. Now facing a possible separation, Faith knew that she had to be strong for her daughter, Savannah. Raising her was a major responsibility and all the healing she ever really needed.

Savannah

Liltera R. Williams

My name is Savannah and I am six years old. My mommy says I am a miracle baby. My daddy doesn't love me...

"Savannah, who were you talking to?"

"Nobody, Mommy."

"You know you can tell me anything, right?"

"Yes, Mommy."

"So who were you talking to? Do you have an imaginary friend?"

"What does imaginary mean?"

"Something that's made up and not real."

"Sunni is real."

"Sunni?"

"Sunni is my friend, but she's not imaginary because I can see her."

"What does Sunni look like?"

"She looks like you, Mommy."

"Savannah, don't be silly."

"She does. She has your eyes, your nose, your lips and she loves wearing red lipstick."

"That's enough. It's time for bed."

"Can I tell Sunni good night first?"

"Go ahead."

"I can't tell her while you're around, Mommy. She won't come out because she's afraid when other people are around."

"Afraid of what?"

"That no one will like her."

"Is that so?"

"Yes, Mommy."

"Well as soon as you tell Sunni good night I want you in bed. Understood?"

"OK. I love you, Mommy."

"I love you too, Savannah."

This can't be happening again. Faith was worried. She knew that young girls had a tendency to talk to themselves or make up fake characters when playing alone, but this Sunni woman kept showing up and she had no idea who she was or what she wanted. First her husband mentioned her and now Savannah. Faith had never seen any ghosts and she prayed over her household every day, so she knew that evil spirits would not make it past the doorstep. Sunni had to be an angel of some sort. Maybe she was protecting Savannah from future heartache. Maybe Savannah knew something that she didn't know, but Faith was scared. She first met her sistas, Sheila and Brenda, when she was around Savannah's age and her mother kept praying them away. But Faith needed them. She needed someone to talk to when her mother and father would argue about money, about him staying out late, about her mother working too much and sometimes about absolutely nothing. Her sistas helped her cope with feeling alone and unimportant, but she soon grew out of the imaginary friend phase. They returned every so often, but Faith no longer paid them any attention. Her father was gone and her mother didn't bother her too much, so she was able to carry on doing just fine. When she was preparing to move out of her mother's home, Sheila and Brenda showed up again and they wanted to follow her, but Faith would not allow it. They weren't mature enough to go where God was taking her, and she didn't want any unnecessary drama distracting her from her dreams. Faith wanted to be an actress. It's ironic that the thought of being someone else stalked her from adolescence to adulthood, but Faith thought it was all a part of her purpose. Now Savannah's showing signs of the same burden. Faith needed to figure out how to keep it from spreading and haunting her daughter beyond its preliminary stage. So she prayed and she prayed some more, but the doubt from wondering if her sistas were resurrected kept creeping into her mind.

Why would God introduce me to them if I was supposed to just let them go?

There was only one way to find out. Faith had to invite them back in. She had to let Sheila and Brenda become a part of her life again or else God wouldn't be able to mend Savannah and the cycle would continue. She needed to figure out how to rekindle their sisterhood, and then end it for once and for all. But where were they? And how would she revive them? Like everything else, Faith began her investigation with a prayer:

Dear God,

As always, I'm coming to you with an open heart and a simple request. Please lead me back to my sistas. Help me carry out your will as you see fit. Forgive me for not obeying my initial assignment. But you know and I know that we all fall short. I'm sorry. I know that my sistas need me. So, God, I'm ready to resume my quest.

Sheila and Brenda had choreographed separate lives of their own, but Faith was prepared to work her way back into their minds and more importantly, into their souls. It was time.

Liltera R. Williams

Sheila

Liltera R. Williams

Chapter 5:
I Should Have Listened

Love me ... Just love me.
All I want is for you to love me ... the way you used to.

Carl hasn't touched me in months. I mean really touched me. Those intimate moments we used to have are now obsolete and scarce. He's always claiming that he's too tired, but he never would have denied my love and affection seven years ago when we first got married. He doesn't even look at me anymore. I've been praying and asking God to give me the strength to leave, but I guess He doesn't hear me. I stopped going to church because the pastor was always snooping in my business — asking me how I'm doing and smiling all up in my face like he doesn't know. I can't stand phony people, especially phony Christians. They say God don't like ugly. I know other women constantly chase after Carl, and I can almost guarantee that he's cheating on me. I don't know why I believe his lies when the truth keeps slapping me right in the face, harder than he did the night I told him I was pregnant. He is nothing but a dog and I am nothing but a fool. My mama once said, "Never trust a man who can't tell you what's on his mind." I should have listened.

Carl communicates best with his fists and there's never much left for me to say after nursing a bruise that takes days, sometimes months, to heal. So we just don't talk much. He sleeps next to me with his back turned and doesn't even offer a consistent "good morning" before he heads to the firm. He's obviously tired of me, but I don't even know why. I wish he would at least offer me an explanation for what I did that made him so angry. He hates me, probably just as much as I hate Brenda. I don't care what Faith used to say about forgiveness. If Carl can't find it in his heart to forgive me for whatever I've done, then why should I forgive her? She's adamant about destroying my life ... trying to damage my reputation by bringing up things that are irrelevant and mundane. I know she talked about me behind my back to Faith. Faith told me everything. I just don't get how someone can be so goddamn hypocritical. Instead of supporting me, she expedites her jealousy and turns on me just because I moved on to a better life. How dare her try to force me be an accomplice for her sleaziness.

A real sista would accept and understand my need to be the total opposite of a Good Samaritan. That's what I love the most about Sunni, my new companion. I wonder what she's doing. I haven't heard from her in so long. She must be ashamed to come around now that she knows what Carl is doing to me. She always knows just what to do to cheer me up, and I need her here with me right now. She's the only one who is able to sense when something is wrong, but I guess she's tired of me constantly putting Carl first. I can't help it. He's the one man who has ever truly cared for me in my state of confusion. I know Sunni understands. She just has a funny way of showing it.

"I understand, Sheila."

"Sunni? I knew you could hear me."

"I always hear you, but you seem to never want to hear me."

"I listen to you all the time, Sunni."

"Yeah, but do you hear me when I'm speaking my mind? I only want what's best for you, Sheila … what's best for us."

"What am I supposed to do? Just run away from the only man who ever loved me?"

"Sheila, you don't get it. Carl does not love you."

"Whatever, Sunni."

"See. My point exactly. You listen, but you never want to hear the truth."

"The only truth is you're jealous because no one loves you the way that Carl loves me."

"You're right, Sheila. I am jealous. I'll continue to be jealous until you open up your eyes. Why can't you love me the way that you love Carl?"

"It's complicated, Sunni."

"What's complicated about loving someone who has always been there for you?"

"Just forget it, Sunni. You will never truly understand."

"Help me understand then, Sheila."

"I can't."

"Why not?"

"Because I don't even fully understand what I'm going through myself."

"Just stop shutting me out. I don't know how much more I can take."

"Well leave like you always do. You and everybody else."

"Why do you always snap at me like that, Sheila? What have I ever done to hurt you?"

"You know what you did."

"Actually, I don't. Please tell me."

"You betrayed me."

"How?"

"Stop acting clueless, Sunni. I know what you're up to and I won't let you win."

"Let me win? I'm not aware of which game we're playing, Sheila."

"Exactly. You like to cheat! But there's no way I'm letting you take what's mine. No way in hell!"

Sheila was on the verge of becoming delusional. Dealing with Carl had made her question Sunni and her real intentions. She knew that Sunni wanted to help, but she was unknowingly making things worse. Sheila didn't like being so paranoid, but her experiences had made her that way. She just wanted to repair things with her husband and all he wanted to do was work late and avoid spending time with her. When he was at home, they argued. And Carl was aggressive. More and more, the tension rose and Carl squelched Sheila's desire with his mounting rage. All she could do was take it, but she looked forward to the day he would love her again, as much as Faith loved to worship and as much as Brenda loved to drink.

Liltera R. Williams

Brenda

Liltera R. Williams

Chapter 6:
Drink Please, Sir!

"Rum and coke on the rocks … and make it snappy!" Brenda demanded the bartender to quickly satisfy her thirst as she took her seat at the bar.

"You're too pretty of a lady to be drinking such strong liquor. How about a long island ice tea instead?" he said to her.

"I know what I want … now give me what I asked for."

"Yes, ma'am."

Brenda had taken solace in becoming a full-time alcoholic and a seasonal man slayer. She could usually be found at a bar drinking her worries away, trying to find a Clark Kent who is looking to transform himself back to Superman. Brenda didn't believe she was worth saving. That's why many of her victims didn't stay around too long.

"So what brings you in here tonight?" the bartender asked as he handed Brenda her drink and attempted to continue the conversation.

"Freewill," she responded.

"Well excuse me if I'm invading your space, but I just wanted to let you know how beautiful you are."

"Heard it all before, Mr. Now do your job and give me a refill." Brenda had already taken a rapid swig of her drink.

The bartender smiled and grabbed her empty glass.

"Coming right up."

I like how speedy he is at serving me. I think I've found my next victim, Brenda thought. Her aggressive nature has never been too much for any man. No matter how many times she pushed them away, they kept on setting themselves up for rejection.

"I'm DeAngelo by the way," the bartender confidently proclaimed while placing Brenda's refilled glass in front of her.

"I'm not interested by the way," she responded without looking up to meet his glance.

"Well, women who play hard to get are my specialty."

Brenda tried to act as if she was slightly irritated and annoyed by his advances. She grabbed her purse and handed him the money for her tab. He looked familiar, but she couldn't remember where she had seen him before. *I'm probably just hallucinating, as usual. Too many drinks tonight, I suppose. It's time for me to call it quits.*

"Good night, DeAngelo," Brenda rose to make her way toward the exit.

"Leaving already? I was just getting started."

"Well if that's how you start, I'd hate to see how you finish."

Halfway to the door and eager to tickle another man's fancy, Brenda looked back to see if DeAngelo was studying her five-foot, nine-inch athletic figure. She was wearing her nude pumps and the shoulder-revealing turquoise dress that she had just bought from Macy's. No panties. Before he could pretend that she didn't still have his full attention, Brenda smiled, rolled her eyes, and left her habitual paradise.

"She'll be back."

He must think I'm drunk and deaf.

"I heard that," Brenda said. His eyes were still stuck on her as she was on the way out. Brenda stumbled to her car, signaled for the alarm to go off and finally made it to where she had parked. Her seatbelt zipped across her and *Songs in A Minor* by Alicia Keys was blasting through the speakers. Track eight, *Jane Doe*. That's who she chose to be on this particular evening, and probably every evening that she reduced herself for a hangover. Even after she sobered up, the previous day's events would not be harkened or negotiated. She contemplated about DeAngelo.

He's fine, but looks don't get me sprung. I wish he was more assertive instead of offering me that weak ass game. He must have thought I was the average female who can't hold her liquor. He'll learn—that's if he's not too fucking clueless to notice that I left my receipt on the counter with his tip and my phone number. The most obvious things are too complicated for a man, but I guess I'll give him the benefit of the doubt and hope that he calls before this sequitur is overturned.

Brenda's patience was wearing thin. The same routine over and over had become a bore and she never remembered exactly what she was partaking in when the next day approached. It was one thing to be intoxicated, but it was another thing to be completely oblivious to what was going on. Brenda had no idea what she was getting herself into.

Sheila

Liltera R. Williams

Chapter 7:
Sistas We Will Be

W hile Brenda was in the process of recovering from her rendezvous, Sheila was still trying to adjust to her new beginning—constantly modifying her daily ritual and trying her best to process and retain every unfamiliar occurrence.

My sistas haven't visited me in so long. I'm stuck in Atlanta, Faith's probably getting her praise on in somebody's church and Brenda still wakes up every day wherever she pleases. It seems like just yesterday we were sitting on my back porch, right before we became teenagers, talking about how happy we were going to be by the time we turned thirty. I celebrated my thirty-sixth birthday two weeks ago and I haven't smiled since the last time I saw Sunni. I hope the journey to happy doesn't have a deadline. I'm having such a hard time keeping up. Brenda, Faith, and I were inseparable back in the day, but somehow we let life interrupt our valuable years of friendship. Faith got married and then she got pregnant. Her husband wanted her all to himself, so he barely let her out of the house unless she was going to church. Brenda hasn't been the same since she started drinking. She thinks it's the only way she can numb the pain. But there's no drink strong enough to make her forget what she's been through.

Never forget where you come from.

My Mama's voice bounced and echoed against the hollowest section of my mind. I was forgetting everything else, but I would never forget the Ville—Jacksonville, Florida. It wasn't much like hell, but it wasn't much like heaven either. I lived there my whole life and never saw much outside of Duval County.

I was often surrounded by death and disappointment. Never thought I would find an escape. At least not until Carl made me move to Atlanta. I hate it here, though. There's nothing but ratchet women roaming around with no purpose. Brenda always told me that I was too bourgeois for the common crowd. I never knew what she meant until I settled in here. I'm on the lookout for something more to sustain me. Writing isn't enough. I'm satisfied with my writing career, but I still don't feel complete. No one reads newspapers anymore and the transition to online media has been an outrageous challenge. Working double shifts as a Staff Writer and Content Editor affords me no time to take care of home. And it seems like I'm just writing just to write, unless it's poetry. Poetry always takes me to a higher ground. I can flow at my own discretion. No syntax rules—just pure, incessant expression. I can go wherever I want to go.

Faith used to tell me that I need to go out and explore the world, but I don't have much of a world if she's not in it. She's too busy praying for other people now and there's nothing I can do about it. She was always telling me to pray for myself, but I haven't heard from her or God lately, so I can't remember how. And Brenda is too wrapped up in her own mess to cover herself in mine. Instead of wasting my time on a man who doesn't love me, I should have been spending more time getting to know my sistas, but it's too late now. We've grown apart and I have to deal with it. I'm already adapting to my new life and there's no such thing as rewinding when it comes to mistakes, but sometimes I do wish that God would consider fast forwarding this stiff life of mine. I'm too crisp to bend and too prosaic for spontaneity. I'm still here, though, and it must be for a good reason. I guess I should thank God for that. Maybe I should try contacting Faith. However, communication works both ways. She usually greets me first, so I guess I'll wait. I may interrupt her need to always tell it like it is. I hate to admit that nine times out of ten she's absolutely right. Her sanctified speeches have slithered past my barriers, and I've been forced to listen to the piercing sounds of her persuasion. Reading the Bible doesn't compare to the firsthand accounts delivered straight from her mouth. God knows my heart. I hope.

Misery loves company and Sheila's misery needed some right about now. A convocation with her sistas was well overdue, but she had evolved so much without them. Backtracking could not mean well for her future—whatever it was made of. Sheila was more than incomplete. She was flawed. Not only due to the constraints of her marriage, but due to her lack of ambition. There wasn't much for her to look forward to. All she had was herself to lean on. And at this point, Sheila didn't have enough admiration for the woman she had become. The adversity was too much and it outweighed the satisfaction of her triumphs. There was no way to balance it all. With a husband that treated her like deadweight, it was no surprise that the load eventually got too heavy. But Sheila tried her best to act like this was a standard way of living, or just existing. As she frequently subjected herself to Carl's abuse, the love she had for herself was expiring at a rapid speed.

Both durable and strong, I can't seem to find an ounce of weakness on the inside of this cushion. Carl knows where to aim. Whether it's an unexpected blow to my stomach, a pinch on my thigh or a tight grip of my arm, my marks are never too much to bear. I hide my blues well. Even when the internal suffering threatens to show its face, I shut it down with a forced smile and a swift goodbye directed toward anyone who attempts to butt their nose in my business. What happens between Carl and me is for us to know and no one else to find out. Some people just can't keep their inquiries hidden. I'm sure my sistas may have a slight idea of what I've been going through since I've hinted at it in the past. Brenda could care less and Faith cannot be found. I'll always have Sunni though, no matter how much I push her away. She keeps on shining, trying to get me to see the light, but to no avail. The last thing I need is for someone else to tell me that I deserve better and that Carl is no good for me. I know my limits. His physical abuse is no different than the sexual abuse that Brenda tolerated from her father. She's constantly judging me—casting stones as if she's unbreakable. We're one in the same. She thinks she has overcome the traps of stupidity, but she's as gullible as they come. I, on the other hand, am quite the contrary. I tune out the naysayers and keep it moving. She just wants what I've got—a man who loves me and takes care of me. I don't care at all about a happy home as long as I have a home to come back to.

Carl is my muse. When you're surrounded by a slew of antagonists, it's necessary to have someone to summon you back to reality. Though my life has been no marvelous phenomenon, it's far from a tragedy. What's tragic is the fact that everyone thinks I'm suddenly losing my mind just because I put up with Carl's temper. They don't know me. They just speculate and assume that what they think they know is the truth. The truth is, I'm OK—an oxymoronic keynote for what most believe to be an immaculate example of a subjective law. Laws were made to be broken. Being married to a lawyer who doesn't abide by the rules has taught me many things;

most importantly, that there's no primary statute for what's acceptable versus what's due for an objection. I've learned to keep quiet and keep still, especially when I can anticipate his rage spewing from a mile away.

"Carl, please don't hit me!"

"Where's Sunni?"

"She ran away again."

"Stop the antics, Sheila. Bring her back!"

"I can't!"

"One..." Carl always counts down before he smites me with successive blows. By now I should be immune to his hostility.

"Two... Three..."

I'm waiting — anticipating the ache of my next tussle with a man who is obsessed with domestication because I have no idea where Sunni is. She sidesteps her way out and vanishes for long periods. I call for her. Carl is still counting.

"Sunni!" She must be shrouded by apprehension. I know she wants to reveal herself. There's no way that she would just opt to watch me be suffocated by my husband. My husband. The man I chose to marry. He owns me. Till death do us part.

"Four..."

I beseeched him to halt, but the counting persisted and then came the blows from his eight fingers and two thumbs.

"Five..."

"Please, Carl! No! Please!"

He pushed me and I skid across the floor. My head broke even with the wall and I was lying there wondering if I was still alive. With his penultimate punch, it felt like a suction of air had been completely extracted from my body. The final blow paralyzed my lungs and I could not breathe. I thought I was a goner, until I heard someone yelling my name.

"Sheila! Sheila! Sheila, wake up!"

It was Sunni. I knew she would come back to see about me.

"Are you alive? Sheila, please say something!"

"Where am I?"

Sunni's voice withered away and I opened my eyes to find my husband kneeling beside me in tears. Sunni was gone, but I needed her to stay, for me and for Carl. However, once again Carl was sorry and once again I was bruised. I've played my position as his punching bag for years now. I solemnly swore to for better or for worse, even when the worse doesn't get any better. It happens over and over again, but somehow I keep ending up subdued by his control. The last time, Carl approached me to check my pulse and walked away after confirming that I was still breathing. This time, he seemed more concerned and regretful. He doesn't usually console me afterwards. If he's having a change of heart, I hope it's not superimposed with the original. I'm sure he doesn't find pleasure in seeing me suffer. He just wants me to be submissive to his restraints and I have trouble complying with the standards he has established. After seven years of marriage, I guess I'm still in training.

Carl eventually stopped sobbing and left my side. When I was sure that he was gone, I walked over to the mirror to inspect my latest stamps of disapproval—a busted lip and a lump underneath my sewed-in tracks that birthed a massive migraine. I needed ice and a quick getaway, but the latter only seems to occur in imaginative phases. I can only pretend that the abuse doesn't happen by converting to Sunni. She radiates through me when I've blacked out and become unconscious. I can bypass all the criticism and navigate my way down a lighted path to rational thinking. Carl likes me to be simpleminded. My opinions don't matter and my well-being is an apparent non-factor. So I fight back by disappearing. If I'm not visible, he can't do much damage. Lord knows he's crippling me. Who am I kidding? I have no idea what the Lord knows. All I know is I don't have enough stability to withstand yet another beat down. My marriage is shaky and I'm senseless when it comes to choosing between a masculine statue that won't bend and a senate member of the feminine species. We can only vote for peace when it's easily attainable and not an illusion for a falsified disposition of camaraderie. I've been in denial for a while now, clashing with my sistas, trying to get them off my back and out of my head. They can't see what I see. Although our bond is like none other, eventually every brand of glue loses its adhesive strength and nowadays we're just fighting to stick together, or fall apart. Brenda and Faith will probably never be accepting of Sunni. They can't even accept the real Sheila. They've cast me out and they wonder why I'm so distant. I can't trust anyone. Not my sistas. Not Carl. Not even myself.

And that's just how it went. Sheila declined responsibility for any misdeeds. All she wanted was happiness. She knew that it would someday catch her by surprise again. If she could speed up the process, she would, but she couldn't and it made her even more pessimistic. There was no turning back and there weren't many incentives for moving forward either. *One day at time*, Sheila thought, but her thoughts were not dependable. As her memory was dwindling, so was her dependence on the conviction of her own truth. Which truth should she believe? Years had gone by and Sheila was still not totally sure about who she was, where she was going or even where she had been. If time heals all wounds, then it must be stalling, and Sheila started to believe that she was contagious. Impatient, segregated and unpleased, she continued to wait. That's really all she could do unless someone, anyone, loved her enough to help her retract and stabilize her amnesia. She needed to recollect from the very beginning. And the abbreviated components of her intuition kept blocking the adequacy of her confirmations.

Chapter 8:
A Stranger's Call

One step forward and two steps back.
I wanna forgive you, but I can't ... I just can't.

S till fading and thriving on a whim of collaborative effort, Sheila's memory was oppressed and in dire need of being restored. She couldn't preserve even the most impactful experiences of her past, but her past still somehow found a way to catch up to her, no matter the rank of her ignorance.

"Hello."

"Hello. I'm trying to reach Sheila Henderson."

"This is Sheila."

"Hello Sheila. How are you?"

"Who is this?"

"Debra."

"Debra?"

"Yes. Your mother."

"How did you get my number?"

"I saved it. I'm sorry to bother you, but I just think we've gone way too long without speaking."

"You have no right to just contact me out of the blue."

"I know, Sheila. I just wanted to hear your voice."

"Since when? You never gave a damn about me!"

"That's not true, Sheila. I always cared about you."

"You know what? Save your announcement and I'll save my sympathy. Goodbye!"

"Sheila, please don't hang up. I just need to know that you're safe. Is Carl still hitting you?"

"What? How do you know about that?"

"You told me about it the last time you called me. You were crying and upset and I calmed you down. You don't remember?"

"No, actually I don't. You're probably lying, which is what you always accused me of when I tried to tell you what your husband was doing to me."

"Sheila, please don't be that way. No matter how many times I say I'm sorry, I know you'll probably never forgive me, but you are still my child."

"Not by choice."

"You have no idea how powerful your words are. They hurt, Sheila."

"Well, I'm glad I'm not the only one hurting."

"Sheila, once again, I'm sorry. I just called to make sure that you're OK. I also have some news that I wanted to share with you, though I doubt that you will even care."

"What news?"

"I have breast cancer and your daddy, well, he's alive and he came back looking for you."

"I don't have a daddy!"

"Sheila, please. Please don't be this way."

"Be what way? The same way you were toward me when I needed you to be my mother?"

"I know I can't make up for things that happened in the past, Sheila, but you can't keep treating me like this. I've tried to reach out to you numerous times."

"Yeah right!"

"It's the truth, Sheila. Not a day has passed when I didn't think of you or wonder if you were safe. You just left without even saying goodbye."

"Say goodbye? There was nothing to say goodbye to. You were never there for me!"

"Sheila, please."

"Please what?"

"Just ... just forget it."

"That's right. Forget it and forgot me!"

Sheila hung up the phone without giving her a chance to say anything else. Although she longed for understanding, she wasn't ready for this immediate confrontation.

She's got some nerve! How could she call me and expect me to be accepting of that bullshit news? She's probably just telling me that to get a reaction out of me. I'll let that foolishness go in one ear and out the other. She thinks it's easy for me to just forget everything she put me through. Carl is the only man I ever loved and the only man who ever loved me back. My daddy wasn't even around to show me what to look for in a potential mate. He left us when I was thirteen and I haven't seen or heard from him since. I've barely seen her since I moved out at eighteen. And now she wants to pretend like she misses me. I don't have time for her superficial act. I have moved on to a new chapter and Carl is the only one welcome to join in and participate. Why is she doing this? Why now? What does she want from me? I'm sure she's glad my so-called daddy is alive. That bastard! What did I ever do to deserve this, God? Things were going just fine. Why can't the past just be the past? I'm sick of it. I'm sick of it all. Just let me breathe!

Breathing no longer came natural for Sheila. She was an undercover suspect in her own scam, gasping for air and trying to decode the message behind the commotion. Everything was moving so fast. Sheila just couldn't keep up with the milestones.

She fell in love with Carl, and then they got married. It was a short courting session, but Sheila instantly knew that he was the one. The verification was in his eyes. He saw beyond her faults and straight into her soul. After years of being promiscuous and trying to establish her self-identity, Sheila needed to be with someone who believed in solidarity. But she could not disclose her secret, at least not while her awareness was still prominent. She did not condone lying, but omissions were suitable in moments that were abstract. Sheila was fulfilled; however, the honeymoon stage diminished with her cognizance. And Carl soon stopped acknowledging anniversaries and accommodating her needs.

When they first left Jacksonville everything was completely fine. Carl opened up a small law firm, and she got her writing job shortly after. It wasn't until Sheila started making silly forgetful mistakes that Carl suddenly started acting different, just like her father.

"Who were you talking to, Sheila?"

"Nobody, Carl. Just my mama."

"I asked you a question, woman."

"I just answered."

"Don't lie to me, Sheila. You know what happens when you lie to me."

"I am telling you the truth, Carl."

"When did you start talking to your mother again?"

"I haven't spoken to her in a long time, Carl. You know that. She just called because she misses me all of a sudden."

"I don't like having people in our business. Casual conversations are nothing short of gossip. What did you tell her?"

"No one is gossiping, Carl. I didn't tell her anything. I barely even talk to her."

"Are you smart-mouthing me?"

"No, I just need some space. That's all."

"Oh, so now you need space? I'm not enough for you? Is that what you're saying?"

"I didn't say that, Carl. I just wish I could move on from everyone and everything from my past. I think my mama finally wants to get to know me. Maybe I should go back home and visit."

"You're not going anywhere. Now go fix me something to eat."

Carl gave Sheila an order, as usual. And as usual, she obeyed. There was no pleasure in refusing. Disobedience only extended her worries.

I wish I could tell him to fix his own damn food and iron his own damn clothes, but I can't ever find the strength to fight back when he hits me. So, I just do what he says. I have valid reasons to believe that all men are the same, so I might as well just take what he can give. No one else is going to treat me any better under these conditions.

Sheila had literally lost all hope. The bad outweighed the good, and there was no telling when it would be vice versa. All she wanted, all she needed, was some peace. She served Carl his dinner and after he finished eating he fell asleep on the couch. Sheila tiptoed to the bedroom to call her mama back. She wanted to find out more about why she was really calling.

"Sorry for hanging up on you. I was upset. Still am."

"It's alright, Sheila. I understand. As long as I can hear your voice, I know that Carl hasn't killed you yet."

"Don't talk like that. No one is dying anytime soon."

"Well, actually, Sheila, I am. My doctor said there isn't much he can do since they didn't catch the cancer early enough."

"What does he mean there's nothing he can do? He's a doctor and doctors heal people. Do you need me to ask Carl to talk to one of his colleagues at one of the hospitals here?"

"No, Sheila. Thank you for the offer, but I don't think so. I don't want your husband dipping into any of my personal business. I'm tired. I can barely remember anything and I keep getting these horrible headaches. You probably have no idea what it feels like. Worrying about you isn't doing me any good either."

"I actually do know what it feels like. I get headaches every time Carl hits me."

"Oh, Sheila. I'm so sorry you have to go through the same thing I went through."

"It's not your fault."

"Yes, it is. I should have left your daddy after the first time it happened. It never stops. You need to save yourself while you still have time."

"Why did you put up with it?"

"I don't know. I was weak. I didn't have any other family members around. Your daddy loved me, believe it or not."

"And Carl loves me."

"Sheila, when a man loves you, he will not hurt you intentionally, especially not to the degree of putting your life at risk. I had to learn for myself that a real man would not treat a woman like his doormat. You see what your father and I went through, how much it almost killed me. If he hadn't left then I would still be suffering as we speak. I wasn't strong enough to walk away, but you are. Sheila, please. Run away and never look back."

"I can't just desert my husband. He's all I have."

"That is not true, Sheila. You have me."

"Since when?"

"Since now."

"I don't need you now. It's too late."

"It's never too late for forgiveness."

"Now, you sound like Faith."

"Are you still talking to your sistas?"

"Sometimes."

"You were always at peace when they were around."

"Yeah, until you prayed them away."

"I had to."

"No, you didn't. You knew how much I needed them."

"Sheila, you needed God more than anything."

"There is no God."

"What did you say?"

"You heard me. If there was a God, then I would not be so miserable."

"You can't blame God for the decisions you've made, Sheila."

"I don't. I blame you."

"I guess that's fair. I pray that you will someday forgive me and finally get some help."

"I don't need help!"

"Sheila, please take it from someone who has been there. I am still your mother. Don't strip that title away from me."

"I'm not stripping anything away from you. Why can't anyone understand that I am perfectly fine and I don't need any help?"

"What if Carl never stops hitting you, Sheila? What if the next time is the last time? What if ... what if I never get to see you again?"

"What if you never forced me to get an abortion? What if you were still blessed to become a grandmother?"

"Excuse me?"

"Rhetorical questions."

"Sheila, am I?"

"Maybe."

"Boy or girl?"

"A girl. Savannah."

"Wow, Sheila. How old is she? When will I get to meet her?"
"She's six and I don't know."

I wanted to tell her never, but I could hear the desperation in her voice. She really was trying to make amends. Am I being selfish? Does she really deserve my forgiveness? I don't even know how to forgive. I muted the phone and wiped away the tears that surged my face with sadness. No matter what we've been through, I honestly can't say that I don't care if I lose my mama. Carl can't stop me from seeing her and he will not stop me from taking my daughter to meet the only other family she could possibly know. Just because Carl doesn't associate with his own flesh and blood doesn't mean that I have to remain isolated from mine. People change, right?

"Mama, hold on, OK? I'll be home as soon as I can. I promise."
"Don't make me any promises that you can't keep."
"I'm going to try my best. No matter what I have to do, I'll be there."
"I hope so, Sheila. It would be nice to see you after all these years and my granddaughter, too. Please call me back tomorrow. I need to get me some rest."
"I will."
"I love you, Sheila. Tell your sistas I said hi. I'm sure you're going to need them after this."

After years of uninterrupted silence, Sheila needed to hear that. She couldn't remember the last time she heard her mother say I love you. It was surreal. Sheila wished she could hug her immediately after that moment. She had never felt the comforting touch from her mother, after an accomplishment or even after bedtime tears. Sheila longed for those embraces ... for an accreditation from the woman who launched her into existence. Being passed over and detached for so many years caused her to scrounge for love in odd zones and she was often snared and discarded. It took its toll on her. She needed validation. Some type of replenishment for all she had endured. Sheila was in a scrimmage with her past, and if her present life was any indication of the outcome, she was for sure that she would lose this challenge.

Carl was standing right behind Sheila when she turned around to place the phone on the hook. He grabbed her by the hair and threatened, "You're not going anywhere." Then he punched her in the face. Only God could truly save her, but she was not ready to mourn over the calamities. It was her own fault. She knew it. She had gotten herself into multiple screw-ups. God would surely laugh at her and dismiss the thought of a renewal. But Sheila had nowhere else to turn. She could not love away Carl's irate behavior and she could not scrape any decency from their leftover feuds. Carl was sick and she was sicker. Sheila loathed the realization that they were made for each other, but there wasn't much that she could do. Reneging on her vows would lead to a total confiscation of her identity, and Sheila was already used to living life as a quadruple threat.

Chapter 9:
Dear God... I'm Sorry

When the righteous cry for help, the Lord hears,
and rescues them from all their troubles.

—Psalm 34:17

The LORD is my shepherd; I shall not want. He maketh me to lie down in green pastures: he leadeth me beside the still waters. He restoreth my soul: he leadeth me in the paths of righteousness for his name's sake. Ye, though I walk through the valley of the shadow of death, I will fear no evil: for thou art with me; thy rod and thy staff they comfort me. Thou preparest a table before me in the presence of mine enemies: thou anointest my head with oil; my cup runneth over. Surely goodness and mercy shall follow me all the days of my life: and I will dwell in the house of the LORD forever. You said if I have faith that you'll take me out of my misery. I'm believing in your Word and holding on for my victory. Guide me, Lord. Amen.

Faith was the strong and humble sista, a woman that Sheila was truly blessed to know. She never complained. However, she had been praying the same prayer every day since she found out her husband was cheating on her. God hasn't answered her yet. Sheila was convinced that Faith's husband was just a low down, dirty, pitiful excuse for a man.

He better be glad he took off before I could get to him.

All the anger she had built up from her own husband using her as his personal punching bag had her wanting to make someone else feel the pain she had been feeling. Faith doesn't deserve to hurt and Sheila felt bad for her. When she asked her why God let this happen to her, Faith responded with, "God doesn't make mistakes. We do."

I guess she's right, Sheila thought.

No matter what's going on, Faith makes sure that she's in church every Sunday. Sheila hadn't spoken to her in a long while, and figured that she should contact her to let her know that she was still breathing. Plus, she had a load of news to share, and she wasn't feeling much exhilaration from the installments in her notebook.

Carl left hours ago and he wouldn't be home anytime soon. Every Sunday, he spends the night with his secret mistress. Sheila was pretty sure that she knew who the mistress was, but she decided not to elaborate on the allegation. Faith never takes long to answer.

"Who's there?"

"Don't act like you're not happy it's me."

"Sheila?"

"Well, it ain't God."

"Don't use the Lord's name in vain. Why haven't I heard from you?"

"I've been tied up."

"I bet. Well it's nice to hear your voice."

"Ditto, Sainta."

Brenda gave Faith that nickname when we were younger. Every time trouble was near, she would always recite a scripture to prove that God was going to forgive us for whatever we did wrong.

"Have you been praying for me?"

"Always, Sheila, but you have to learn how to pray for yourself as well. God won't save you unless you open up your own mouth and ask."

"I guess, but you know you're His favorite child."

"We're all God's favorite, Sheila. Is something wrong? You don't usually reach out to me unless something is wrong. What is it?"

"I have bad news and worse news. Which one do you want to pray over first?"

"Just tell me, Sheila. I'll pray over them both at church. You're going to make me late."

"Well, yesterday my mama called to tell me that she has breast cancer and as soon as I hung up the phone, Carl gave me another black eye."

"Oh, no, Sheila. I'm so sorry to hear that."

"It's OK, Faith. You know I've been through it all. I can handle anything."

"Sheila, you have to stop thinking that you're Superwoman. Let go and let God. His power is like no other."

"No offense, Faith, but I don't want to hear you brag about how good your God is right this moment."

She always gets upset when I dismiss her holy talk, but she knows how hard it is for me to believe in the God she serves.

"OK, Sheila. Well, what are you going to do?"

"I don't know, Faith. I don't know. Just keep praying and call me back when your God answers."

"You know I will. But He's your God, too, Sheila. Maybe if you started giving Him a little more of your time, you wouldn't have to deal with so much."

"Maybe. I've tried it and it never works. Prayer isn't for everybody."

"It's for anybody who wants it … anybody who believes."

"I believe that we need to change the subject."

"John 3:16."

"Oh come on, Faith … not the scripture recital."

"For God so loved the world that He gave his only begotten son that whoever believes in Him shall not perish but have everlasting life."

"Faith, I've always respected your opinion, but that doesn't mean I have to accept it."

"Why do you ask me for advice if you know that you will never consider applying it, Sheila? My viewpoint hasn't changed. God is the head of my life. Maybe if you situated Him as the head of yours, you wouldn't have to make me the successor of your downfall."

"I said I respect your opinion."

"Respecting it is not enough if I'm wasting my knowledge and my worry on someone who doesn't truly want to be rescued. You should probably contact Brenda. I'm sure she can help you with your new dilemmas better than I can."

"You know Brenda hardly ever listens."

"Well, I don't blame her, Sheila, It's time for you to be the bigger person. If Brenda won't change, then maybe you should."

"Why do I have to be the one to initiate it?"

"Because God said so."

"And what book of the Bible can I find that rule in?"

"Here comes the sarcasm. As if you're going to open it up and read it, anyway."

"I might."

"And I might believe you. I have to go, Sheila. Contact Brenda and be nice."

Sheila wasn't in the mood to engross her hellos and goodbyes with a cursive signature. They would be misaligned and misplaced on purpose. She didn't want to contact Brenda and she didn't want to resolve their dispute, but Faith was right. It was time for her to be the bigger person … to reach out to her vigilante and render a solution for their incompatibility. They couldn't go on forever acting like this — blaming each other for their binary deficiencies and not confronting the issues at hand.

It was finally time for the intervention — a one-on-one brawl with her fellow counterpart. Brenda was already cocked and loaded.

Brenda

Liltera R. Williams

Chapter 10:
Silence Kills

I wonder what God was thinking when He said that we should forgive those who trespass against us. It's hard to forgive a liar, a cheater, or even a filthy child molester. My whole life has been fucked up because of what my so called daddy did to me. How am I supposed to just forgive and forget? Forgiveness isn't free. That bastard better be glad that he's dead. If he was alive, I'd kill his ass again. I need a drink … a strong one with no chaser. Who's calling me? Sheila? What could she possibly want? I don't feel like talking. Go away! I'll just ignore her.

"Hello! Brenda?"

She won't keep it up for long. I don't know why she's bothering me. It's been months since we've talked. I don't have time to listen to her complain. She's always complaining. She's so ungrateful. She doesn't have the right to fuss about any of her blessings because that's what they are, straight from God's hands to hers. I wish she would just leave me alone.

"Brenda, I know you're there!"

"What do you want, Sheila?"

"Why are you always so irritated with me? I bet if it was Faith calling you'd be eager to talk."

"You are absolutely right, my sista. You only call on me when you want something. So what is it?"

"That is not true and you know it."

"Truth be told, I don't have much time to chat. Hot date at seven."

"Who is it this time?"

"As always, that is none of your business."

"You don't tell me anything anymore, Brenda."

"Yeah, because you always run back and tell Carl everything. He is your man, not mine, and my business should always remain between me and you. You still fail to understand that."

"I don't tell him everything."

"And I am a virgin who has never tasted alcohol. What is it, Sheila?"

"Just forget it."

"See what I mean? You're so damned timid. Spill!"

"My mama called."

"Did you answer?"

"Yes. We talked for about five minutes."

"You actually talked to her? And for five minutes? That bitch does not deserve a second of your time."

"She is not a bitch, Brenda."

"She will always be a bitch to me."

"So, do you care to hear what she had to say?"

"Slightly. What did she want?"

"She called to tell me that she has breast cancer and that my daddy is looking for me."

"Wait … what? Well, isn't this a double shocker! So your mama is dying and your daddy is still alive?"

"Seems that way."

"Did you tell Faith?"

"Of course I did."

"What was her response?"

"She recited a Bible verse, told me to pray, of course, and then to reach out to you."

"Well, I am certainly appalled. There's got to be more to it than that."

"I don't know."

"What do you mean you don't know? You didn't ask?"

"No. I was too angry … too shocked"

"You still should be. What else do you have to tell me?"

"Carl hit me again."

"Nothing new. I hope you hit him back this time."

"It won't do me any good."

"Why not? He's a bitch, too. One good smack in the balls should deliver the message that you are fed up with his controlling ass. Come on, Sheila! Why are you still putting up with his bullshit?"

"I'm not like you, Brenda."

"Obviously."

"See, this is exactly why I don't like calling on you. You always find a way to make me feel worse. I should have just kept it all to myself."

"Look, Sheila, your problems are not my problems. As your sista, it is my duty to listen to you complain about your scum of a husband, but I will not let you reel me in. You can't change him, but you can change yourself. Men don't react to pain. They react to threats and action. I'm not like you, either."

"What's that supposed to mean?"

"I'm carefree, bold and independent. You're shy and reserved and on the verge of being a dead woman if you don't get out now. Sheila, you know how I feel about any man who puts his hands on a woman. He's a coward."

"And you're a hoe. Nobody's perfect, Brenda."

I knew she would go there. She always does. I can't stand it when she tries to use my own ammunition against me, but I have the upper hand. I always win.

"My therapist told me to pause and pray whenever I think I'll get angry, so I'll just pretend like you didn't say that."

"You're seeing a shrink?"

"Yes, Sheila. Don't act as if you've never consulted with someone else to help you make sense of your issues."

"I don't have any issues, Brenda."

"And I don't have tits. Sheila, stop being so fucking naïve."

"Don't curse at me."

"Don't lie to me."

"What exactly is it that I'm lying about this time?"

"What do you *not* lie about, Sheila? You're so full of bullshit it's a shame."

"For the last time, Brenda, do not curse at me. I'm not one of your playthings. You can't control me with your domineering tone. Show me some respect."

"Respect? Let's not talk about respect, Sheila. You're the last person who deserves respect from me."

"You know, Brenda, you're a piece of work."

"Piece of work. Piece of shit. Whatever you want to call me, I'll be it. But one thing I'll never be is stupid."

"I should have listened to Faith when she told me to abandon you."

"Faith didn't tell you to abandon me. She probably told you to repent. And this is my cue. Don't come crying to me every time Carl hits you. Call on Faith with that bullshit from now on. My hoe ass is currently unavailable."

I ended the conversation knowing that she wanted me to keep listening. Even in the midst of her anger, I knew that she was reaching out for help, but it wasn't my fault that she was hurting. She was trying to shift the blame. First sign of denial. I know it all too well.

Chapter 11:
Stop Singing that Sad Song

I can't keep up with the melodies. The music is too loud and the lyrics are too jumbled. I need a translator—someone to decrypt the syncopated sounds and substitute this selection with one that includes more staccato mixtures. The beat is too unsteady. I want to dance on cue, not at this wild tempo. Control is essential. I need to be able to control my steps. Don't need anyone else mimicking my groove. That moment when you hear the high note above the strings, it's my verbal sign language and I'm telling you to run for cover. I want to protect you ... protect us from the diluted gospel, so I'm pulling myself out of the choir. No more singing off key. I've captured the tone of this ballad and it's another sad love song that has smeared its way into my heart. I don't want to samba and I don't want to salsa; I just want to stand here and let this instrumental guide me until I am able to segue through to the last successional belt of emotion.

Music is all I've ever really needed to get by. I can shake off the torment and shrug away the tribulations of yesteryear. No one can bother me when I'm occupied with hymns that take me back to that old school feeling. Listening to music allows me to reminisce about the disasters in a historical mode.

"Brenda, open up," Daddy demanded.

"Please hurry," I yelled, right before the door flew open and caused me to drop the phone.

"Brenda, baby ... I'm so sorry." Daddy was kneeling before me, crying, and I didn't know what to do. I needed Mama to show up right then and there.

"Liar! Why did you do that to me?"

"I don't know what came over me. You're so beautiful. I wanted to show you how much I love you."

That was his answer ... his reason for taking advantage of me and stealing my innocence. But this would be the last time. I was ready for it to stop.

"You said you would never do it again! I believed you!"

"Brenda, I'm so sorry. Please don't tell your mama."

"Get out!" I yelled and scurried past him to make my way to the kitchen. He soon followed, still weeping and begging me to forgive him. I was scared, so I grabbed a knife and told him to keep his distance.

"You wanna kill me? Go ahead. I deserve it," he said.

"Just stay away from me."

He ignored my words and continued to walk toward me. I stuck the knife out hoping that he would stop, but he didn't. Not until his chest was touching the sharp end of the knife.

"Go on. Do it," he dared me.

I stood there contemplating, wondering if I should. Daddy quickly grabbed my wrist. "I said do it," he insisted.

My grip became tighter.

"Why did you do that to me?" I asked again.

He didn't answer me. He just looked at me and simply said, "I'm sorry."

"Well, I don't accept your apology." I drew my hand back and lunged the knife forward. Daddy jumped, but he wasn't quick enough. I successfully connected with his flesh. The knife was sticking out of his side. He looked down at it and then back up at me.

"Brenda... I... I'm..."

"Don't speak. Just go!"

"Help me, Brenda. Please. You don't want me to die, do you?"

I didn't mean to stab him. I just wanted to scare him so that he wouldn't touch me again. I didn't mean to. I really didn't mean to.

Sheila

Liltera R. Williams

Chapter 12:
Day by Day I Pray ... Until It Starts to Rain

The sun has been shining all day. No matter how hard I pray for rain, God keeps giving us these beautiful afternoons. But there's nothing beautiful about life when you're constantly counting teardrops and hoping that you're going to wake up to see the next sunrise. When Carl asked me to marry him, I felt like I was in heaven. Now, I can't escape this hell I'm in. I don't know what I did to deserve this kind of treatment. He claims that he still loves me, but he sure has a funny way of showing it. Two days ago he came home smelling like another woman, and had the nerve to ask me to rub his back. I only did it because I couldn't take any more of his punches. There aren't enough Band-Aids in the world to cover all the scars he's given me, inside and out. I'm not dead yet, so I guess God is trying to tell me something. I tried praying the way Faith taught me this morning and even asked for forgiveness. I don't think I'll ever forget what Carl has done to me, but hopefully someday I'll be able to move on and enjoy some happy days like I used to have. And maybe then I won't have to keep hoping for signs to fall from the sky. The telepathic interconnection I had with my sistas has dulled and eliminated itself from the proximity of our attachment. Faith and Brenda don't always respond to my probes for comprehension. I've been trying extremely hard to recycle the segments of our compound alliance, but sometimes I guess I need to be left alone.

"I can do bad all by myself ... I can do bad all by myself," Sheila repeated as she combed through her tangled weave and stared at her reflection in the mirror. But the fact of the matter is she was terribly afraid of being alone. Carl is the one who saved her from loneliness. When they first met on that cold winter evening in December, Sheila had no idea that things would turn out to be the way they are now. The generous gentleman who offered her his jacket after caressing away the goose bumps on her arms, turned into a lousy coward who strokes his ego daily with each punch he inflicts on her flesh. Thirty-three trips to the emergency room, six black eyes later, and Sheila just can't seem to let go. Carl still has not delivered any meaningful *sorrys*. They all have become casually repetitious at this point. He is weak, and a coward like Brenda said, but Sheila is even weaker. It would be easy for her to walk away, if she didn't feel like she had nowhere to go. Sheila has accepted suffering as her only choice, but she is quietly awaiting a reliable and safe proposition.

"How much longer are you going to stick around and allow Carl to treat you this way, Sheila?"

"I've already told you that it's complicated, Sunni."

"What's so complicated about walking away?"

"Walking away to what? A life with you? I can't do that. No one will accept us together, Sunni. You know that."

"I guess you're right, Sheila. We're two different people. You've changed. Just a year ago you were ready to run away with me, but Carl always seems to win you over. Why, Sheila? What does he have that I don't have?"

"Just drop it, Sunni."

"No, Sheila. I'm tired. I'm tired of waiting for you to reach your breaking point. I deserve more than this."

"You're right, Sunni. You do. But what am I supposed to tell Carl and everybody else for that matter? I fell in love with a woman who wants to set me free? That's ridiculous, Sunni, and you know it. We can't run away together, so just take me as I am or find the next exit. I was just fine before you came along and I'll be just fine if you decide to go."

"I'm not going anywhere, Sheila. We're meant to be together. Carl can't control our fate. When you're ready to let him go, I'll be here, but I'm not sure how much longer I can stand by and watch him hurt you."

"This is my life, Sunni. Just go. I'm no good for you."

"No, Sheila. You're no good for yourself."

Carl

Liltera R. Williams

Chapter 13:
A Man's Shame

Sheila knew I was a womanizer when she met me. Even after seven years of manipulating and controlling her, she still hasn't managed to rectify my ways. I know she recognizes my weaknesses, but I feel sorry for her. More than I do for myself. I keep telling her not to make me angry. I don't mean to hit her, but she keeps doing things to piss me off. She must know I love her because she hasn't left yet. She's not going anywhere. Who else is going to take care of her like I do? She should be satisfied that I care enough to come home, especially after the way Sunni has been treating me lately. Sheila has never made me feel the way Sunni does. But Sunni can't do all the things that Sheila can do, either. That's why I need them both. Sheila loves running Sunni away, though. She has no idea that I always know where to find her.

Why are women so insecure? Men don't like games. We don't waste time playing Solitaire when we're holding all the spades. That's all I'm saying. Sheila knows the deal, and I share my cards between her and Sunni sparingly. I deserve to have the best of both worlds. I know Sheila may not be happy with my decision to leave her sitting lonely on Sunday nights, but she handles it like a big girl. I can't ask for much more than this. I may be a bit selfish at times, but God knows I mean well. He knows I only want what's best for Sheila, but I have needs, too. Who's going to take care of me when she does finally decide to leave? I don't even want to imagine that. I'll get it together sooner or later.

I just don't know how to love Sheila as much as I have grown to love Sunni. She understands. She always does. I can't even blame her if she wants to go. I assume she's having her cake and eating it, too, just like I am. Probably with extra sugar on top. That's a sweet tooth for my ass. Damn. I've heard all about karma, but I have no desire to meet her anytime soon. I'm totally satisfied with what I've got, even if I am double dipping. I'm just doing what I have to do; every man for himself. If Sheila wasn't so standoffish and shared more about her past with me, then maybe I could relate to her more, but all she does is shove her feelings into her notebooks, and holds them hostage like I can't have access to her emotions. I tried to be a good man for her, but she's turned me into a handicap. I know she has issues. So do I. In the beginning Sheila was proficient and versatile. Now, she's just reeking of despair. I can't love her this way ... not while she's fractured and staggering to get by. I want her to be conditioned to subscribe to my authority. She keeps running, so I have no choice. Falling in love with Sunni was not deliberate; it was accidental. If only Sheila could annul her perception of our suspicious romance. We would all be satisfied.

Sheila

Chapter 14:
So, Now What?

Mama takes it and I have to take it, too
When daddy beats Mama,
I don't know what to do
but I have to come to her rescue
I can only become Superwoman
when it pertains to me
If I drown in her tears,
who's gonna care enough to see
that I was only trying to help
and I can't save my Mama all by myself...

My daddy was a bastard and he never understood what it meant to be a father, but Mama gave him chance after chance anyway. A man is going to do what you allow him to do, and he's never going to ask you how you feel about it, because he's a man. Sometimes I wonder if Carl still loves me. Sometimes I wonder if I even love myself. Why can't time be reversed when we're ready to make a change? I wish I could start over. I'd ask God to let me be raised by a single parent, because most marriages don't last. No more grudges. I know Mama didn't mean it. It's all Daddy's fault. I want to forgive her. God could have saved me the benefit of being raised in a two-parent household because it was all just a front. Normal doesn't mean healthy, and that's probably why I feel so sick. The beautiful memories of my past were swiped away with a smoking gun that was fired before I could even take a deep breath. Now, I exhale every time I get a chance. I probably would have even settled for a stepdad, but Mama loved Daddy way too much. More than she could ever love me. He was her Superhero, and never even did much to try to rescue her.

He punched her when she would ask him a sincere question. Said she was talking back. The same saga continues with me and Carl. He told me he was sorry for the hundredth time last night. I know he didn't mean it, so I held him as he cried, with tears drowning my bosom and shattering my exposed heart. For the first time in a long time, I felt needed. It was as if I finally mattered. But this scar on my shoulder is a constant reminder of his deceit. I can't ignore it and I'll never be able to erase the residue of its smothering presence. It aggravates me to the core, and I know he'll never understand, like I always do, no matter how many times he shatters my heart. Sometimes I wonder how my mama was even able to survive.

There's always a warning before the storm comes. I ignore it because I've become stagnant to change. I want things to stay familiar. There's no happiness to be found after disruption has slaughtered all possibility of a sinister confession that becomes invisible with time. When will I heal? Dear God, I know you're always listening, but why don't you ever respond in a way that I can be sure that it's you? How am I supposed to know if I'm doing the right thing? You're always hiding from me. Have I sinned that much? I'm sorry. I really am. And I'm not just saying it so you can set me free. I'm saying it because I really mean it. I want to change. I want Carl to love me the way that he loves Sunni and I want my sistas to understand that sometimes I just need to be alone. I want everyone to stop treating me like this sad case. I know that I'm fighting a battle, by my sporadic nature was never planned. You and I both know that, God, so why won't you help me? Help me show the whole world that you made me this way and make them accept me for who I am. God? Please answer me. I'm tired of talking to myself and it's rude to ignore someone when they are addressing you. God? Please, God. Please take me out of this misery and remove this stronghold because it has done nothing but rupture the faith I'm storing underneath. God, if you're really listening, I want you to know that I forgive you. I forgive you for cursing me to a life of shame. I forgive you for not making me strong enough to handle this spotlight that only burns with more reminders of my weak spots. I cannot continue fighting against an opponent who never shows me any mercy, so, God, I suggest you show up sooner rather than later because something has got to give.

Chapter 15:
Sistas Forever

I remember the last time Faith, Brenda, and I were all together at once. We toured downtown Atlanta and Brenda kept telling me how sadity I was because I was turning my nose up at the scenery. I've been in Atlanta for a while now, and the Underground Station has never been my favorite spot. Before we got trapped in the streets of the south, we had lunch at Gladys Knight's Chicken and Waffles. It was my first time visiting. Carl always took me to the exquisite restaurants on the other side, but GCW was well-known as a southern taste sensation. I could care less about how snooty my sistas thought I was being. I just knew I deserved the best of the best, especially considering where I come from.

"I think I'll order The Super Southern Sampler with the fried green tomatoes."
"And what would you like to drink, ma'am?"
"Half coffee, half creamer please. Lots of sugar."
"No problem. Be right back."
"You still eat like a bird, Sheila."
"And you still talk shit like one, Brenda."
"Censor the cuss words, please."
"Loosen up, Faith."
"I'm loose enough. I'm here, aren't I?"
"Where would you rather be?"
"In heaven begging God to let you both in."
"I know I'll make it in. Brenda is the one who needs to repent for all of her sins."
"Very funny."

It felt good to release some tension, but I knew our subtle moment wouldn't last very long. Brenda always found a way to ruin the moment and Faith's intervening wasn't always effective.

"Hold on, y'all. Carl is calling."
"Uh oh. Better go check in with your master."
"Brenda, please don't start."

"She's always jumping when he calls. We never get to finish our sista sessions. I wish she would just divorce that bastard and find somebody better."

Brenda and I could never agree on the true meaning of happiness. For me, it was financial security. For Brenda, it was freedom. I shouldn't have told her about Carl abusing me the first time. She'll never accept him because of it. It reminded her too much of her own past … the way her father treated her mother. I guess she knows all about the firsthand repercussions, but I don't care to hear her opinion. She's always so critical of my decisions and never takes the time to analyze her own.

"She needs to wake up and realize that a man who beats you can't possibly love you."

This was an ongoing battle — me and Brenda going at it with Faith playing the mediator.

"She'll learn soon enough. I look too good to let a man treat me any kinda way. I don't know why she keeps pretending to be down just to spend more time with us when she'd rather be sitting with the rich folks at Sugarloaf discussing the latest in sold-out trends."

Once again, I would have to put her in her place.

"You think you're all that with your chinky eyes, your natural hair and your fake ass accent. You are nobody special!" I was furious. Before Brenda had a chance to retaliate with even more hurtful words, I was already standing, prepared for whatever this new argument would lead to.

"Come on, y'all. It's not that serious." Faith hated being in the middle of our spats.

"No, I'm sick of her thinking she's better than everybody."

"I don't think I'm better than anyone, Brenda. You just don't know how to act civilized in public. Why can't you just let bygones be bygones?"

"Because you are ashamed of where you come from, Sheila. Face it and then admit the truth."

"Ashamed of what, exactly? Ashamed of the fact that I respect myself enough not to answer to the street call, 'Shawty'? That I'm classy enough not to wear butt-length sew-ins with outrageously colored weave attached to my scalp? Or ashamed of my shape and that I'm too much of a professional to wear skinny jeans so that I can trick myself into believing that I've lost an unbelievable amount of weight. Get real, Brenda!"

"That is exactly what I am talking about. You don't appreciate where you come from."

"I appreciate it. I just don't dwell on my past as much as you do."

"Whatever, Sheila. I don't dwell on anything. I just know better than to let a man control me. You let Carl run you like a slave. I don't have time for this!"

"I'd rather let one man run me instead of letting a million men run through me!" I know those words stung her. She wanted more than anything to have a man that would love away her pain — someone who wouldn't judge her by her past and would treat her like she mattered. She was jealous of me. Even though Carl was an asshole, he still took care of home, and Brenda no longer knew where home was.

"Why do you two do this every time we get together?"

"I don't know, Faith, but I gotta go. My husband is waiting for me at home."

"Your husband is just like my daddy!"

Brenda just couldn't let it go. I walked past the waitress as she was returning to the table. "Is everything OK, ma'am?"

"Yes, everything is perfectly fine. Please cancel my order."

Liltera R. Williams

Chapter 16:
Period at the End of Every Sentence

A pen and pad was all I ever really needed to record the permanent memories of abuse and neglect. Brenda is right. For the past seven years I have been Carl's slave, standing at attention during every beck and call, ready to obey his next command. *Iron my shirt, Sheila. Wash my good pants. Cook me dinner. Shave my chest. Reschedule my doctor's appointment. Rub my back. Fix my tie ...* and a bunch of other authoritative demands. Carl is the daddy I never really had. Part of me loves feeling so needed. The other part hates feeling so used. But there is no bargaining with Carl. He's a successful lawyer who can argue his way out of any criminal offense. The first time he ever hit me, he easily convinced the officer that it was an accident, and threatened to kill me if I ever called the police again.

On a good day, he simply yells at me for doing something wrong. The food was too cold. He couldn't find the remote. The bed wasn't made. I forgot to pay the mortgage. It seemed like the only thing that I could do right was make love to him. In those passionate moments, Carl became a completely different person. He caressed me like I was important, kissed me with an intense force of appreciation, and stroked me gently as if he would never hurt me. And then he snapped out of it when he realized that I was not Sunni. Every day is a new struggle for survival, as Carl smothers my pleas with repeat apologies that are only sincere for a moment, until the next time he gets angry with me and runs away to find her.

What am I going to do? I don't want to leave Carl, but I can no longer take the abuse and constant embarrassment of the scars he paints on my body that I cover up so that people can't see. I am broken ... in a faraway city with no support system. I need my sistas here all the time, but they can't seem to understand my dilemma. While most women would run in fear after the first physical blow, I know how important it is be loyal. Carl is my husband. I made a vow to love him for better or for worse, and I believe the worse will get better soon. And if it doesn't, I will just pray to the God that Faith is always talking about, even if He won't listen. I don't want to waste the Master's time, but if He's real, I sincerely want help ... or at least help for Carl. He's the one who is sick. Though I try to help him heal, my forgiveness medicine isn't enough for the disease that possesses him. *I'm sorry, Sheila. I won't hurt you again.* Empty, repetitive promises are now the norm. I have grown use to his false declarations to change.

If the day should ever come, I will probably be too damaged for repair. No other man would be able to pick up the pieces of my shattered ego. Carl has become an animal, and I have grown too afraid to tell him *no*. Being with him is easier than being without him, and loneliness is not for me. The company of silence mixed with the urge of desire would only result in an explosion of regret, and I can't handle that kind of stress. Mistakes are not my forte. Forgiveness is now a routine practice and I'm still trying to learn exactly how it goes. Every day there is something new for me to separate from the old, but my scrapbook is continually running out of pages.

Sunni

Liltera R. Williams

Chapter 17:
There She Goes Again

There she goes, walking with a slight twist, repositioning her hair on key with sly arm gestures and smiling at total strangers as they pass her by. I can't keep my eyes off of her. There is something special about this woman. No other female specimen has ever captured me so intently. This is a destined attraction. But how am I going to gain her long-term attention? Right now she isn't interested in getting to know me because her husband won't let her. I ignore all negative possibilities and continue to watch her stroll along on her daily path. I know she knows I'm watching. Why won't she look up? If I could just briefly catch her glance, I know she would instantly feel my desire to take her away from the man who is causing her so much pain. Is she afraid of the sun? I know I can make her smile and maybe she can make me dance again. I've spent too many nights alone, wondering what it feels like to be loved by her. To love without a limit is such an exclusive endeavor, but I know she's worthy and so am I. It's obvious that she's hurting, but she looks so confident. I hope she'll let me in soon. I'm sure she's just as smart as those articles she writes for the Atlanta Tribune. I've also read every poem she has posted in her creative column. *Something that Starts with an S* is my favorite:

I'm waiting for something ... something that starts with an S. Is love really in the air? Or is it incomplete, inconclusive, in medias res? Because I can't seem to find it underneath the crest while searching for the rest of me — the missing ingredients for this recipe of completion. He told me I'm too good to be true and got me to thinking. Am I really that rare? I wear weave in my hair. My car has a spare. I work for a living. I'm caring and giving. Glasses fit tight. Spell check when I write. Say my prayers before I go to sleep every night. So what is it that's so different about my personal life? The truth is I'm too good to be single and average is too easy. I will not settle for a man who will leave me when too good to be alone is blowing up his phone. Love is too precious. I need someone to view me as too good to be helpless and rescue me today. Someone who is too good to let go when I'm ready to walk away. Single and successful is too sad. I want him to want me so bad that he won't become too blind to let me walk past. Someone who will catch me real fast when I jump through hoops. Someone too good to be blue because red is my favorite color. Someone who is too friendly to only be my lover. Someone who understands the struggle of a woman who wants a mate who isn't too afraid to be great. This is an SOS for cardiac arrest. I need someone who isn't too lazy to try their best. Are you that someone? Someone who can make me smile too much and melt when you touch my skin. Someone who will let me sneak my way in and study your grin as I introduce you to joy's identical twin who answers to the name Happy. Will you slap me with the kind of Scooby Shaggy interaction I crave? I'll be your slave and won't be too bad to behave. If you're too good to be seen, I'll smother my face in my pillow and hope to find you in my dreams. I know you must exist. There's no way I'd be feeling like this if I wasn't sure that you will be revealing yourself soon. My heart has saved room for you. So what are you going to do? Keep hiding in the shadow of the stars or finally show me who you really are? If you're too close to be too far and I'm too simple to be too hard, then why haven't you discovered me yet? Are you too dry to be wet? No Sweat. I'm too smart to forget what I've been promised. If you're not too ashamed to be honest, then tell me the truth or am I too bulletproof for your affection? Are you too lost to seek direction? Let me know. I'm tired of being too lonely to grow. I need something ... someone who isn't too slow to go when my busy days have stopped.

I wish I could be that someone, or that something that she's looking for. I'll always try my best to tell her the truth, but she must not be too blinded by her own imagination to see it. She seems to live in a fairytale world, but this is real life. I hope she wakes up before it's too late, because I'm standing right here, right in front of her.

Brenda

Chapter 18:
Sexy Cognac Crush

Men don't think. They just react to what makes them feel good. DeAngelo was exactly what I expected him to be. When he saw my number on the back of the $100 bill I gave him, I knew it wouldn't take long for him to call. I was ready for him to show me just how much he loves women who play hard to get ... and just how hard I could get him.

"Hey, beautiful. I knew you wanted me."

"Is that so?"

"Very much so. Now, when can a brotha get some play?"

"Well, I'm not into games ... but if you're prepared to satisfy my needs, meet me at the Hilton at seven. Room 2408. I'll be waiting."

"Naked, I hope."

I'm sure he was flattering himself just seconds after I hung up the phone. I'm keen on conducting business in extravagant settings. Prostitutes get down anywhere, no matter the circumstances, but I'm a professional. I've gone thirteen full days without sex and I'm feening for an orgasm—one that will last me until my next adventure.

DeAngelo arrived at the hotel seven minutes before seven and I was ready. I invited him into the room after his first knock, and we immediately began to engage in our sexcapade. He stripped me of the white robe I was wearing to find the firm, properly situated nipples of my C cup breasts and a neatly shaved vaginal hairline underneath. He then lifted me onto the bed and began to place soft kisses all over my Love Spell scented skin, from the heels of my toes to the inner crevices of my thighs. I was automatically aroused. I positioned myself to carefully remove his shirt and the khaki slacks he was wearing. His freshly shaved, slanted penis was now staring me in the face. I estimated that it would measure about ten inches if straightened. Experience has made me a dickmatician.

"Put it in your mouth," DeAngelo demanded. I've always been good at following directions, but when it comes to men and my spontaneous pleasure activities, I like to be the one in control. I tried to skip out on his request by attempting to rise from the bed, but I ended up gifting him with my famous in and out technique for about forty-five minutes. He was into it ... so into it that he didn't want me to stop.

"Call me Daddy," he ordered.

"I don't have a daddy and I'm tired of sucking your big ass penis!" I snapped. I was immediately irritated by his demands.

"Hurry up and make me come so that you can get the hell out of here!" DeAngelo obliged. He stroked me long and hard. His rough penetrations reminded me of the moment when I was twelve and helpless, but I had grown to like it rough. DeAngelo rested for a brief second after his final stroke, removed himself from inside of me, and disposed of the worn condom.

"Thanks for the nut," he said before slamming the door. *Men ain't shit!* I need a drink.

Tears started to flow down Brenda's cheeks as she prepared herself for a hot shower. Room service would soon be on the way with her double glass of Hennessy and Coke, and she needed it bad. Brenda had lost count of the number of men that journeyed through her tainted sea. One for every year of her existence times two she guessed. Aaron, Chad, Bruce, and DeAngelo were the last four. She couldn't remember the names of most of the others, but her daddy was the first. The first man she ever trusted damaged her completely, and since then, she hasn't trusted any of the men that she has granted permission to take her to an orgasmic height. She simply just learned to enjoy the ride, and she never forgot to put on her seatbelt.

Faith

Chapter 19:
God Said It, and It Is So

OK, God, show me a sign. I don't know how much further I can stretch my faith. You said you would never forsake me. I need you now...

I've never been desperate enough to chase a man. When my husband found me, I knew it was destiny knocking at the door with fate tagging right along. He followed me from the gas station all the way to church. After I introduced myself with a hesitant smile and unmatched eye contact, he immediately asked for my number. He wouldn't even tell me his last name, but any man who was that determined to make me smile had a chance at winning my heart. I gave him my number and went on to worship.

The topic of that night's Bible study session was *Never Give Up*, an ironic forecast for what he had, in fact, done when it came to the love we worked so hard to establish seven years ago. I gave him all I had and he still keeps leaving me for a modern version of the woman I will never fully become. I forfeited my independence to appease his need to execute his manly duties and his obsession with being the sole provider of a household that I worked so hard to maintain. I love him too much to hate him and God won't allow me to seek worldly revenge. Although I may not understand the reasoning behind this unexpected heartbreak, I know that He will bestow an adequate form of punishment for my husband's decision to neglect me to participate in an adulterous fling. God's karma is the most satisfying form of payback. While He's busy healing my heart, my husband is sure to reap what he sows. I have vowed to never put another man before God again, and when my husband finally realizes his mistake, I will have already forgiven and forgotten the pain.

Happy can only be found in God. It is not a temporary fix, but a permanent supply. Go after your happiness. Success takes work, fortitude and effort. Success happens when opportunity meets preparation. The secret of our success is found in our daily agenda. Schedule your appointment with joy and don't be late. Never give up!

Pastor made his statement with such assurance, as if I was the only one he was talking to and my satisfaction was his number one concern. I want to get to happy, but I know I can't make it there alone.

Sheila

Liltera R. Williams

Chapter 20:
Poetry ... Speak It!

My heart can't speak so it silently shouts
Unheard, hollow echoes fill the space around me
Quiet that fades with each whisper

Men come and go, but if you give them too much of your power, they will leave you with absolutely nothing. I had to learn the hard way. After enduring so many years of Carl's cheating and abuse, I forgot what real love looks like, what it feels like, what it sounds like, and how it's supposed to last. If any other man were to come along and try to sweep me off my feet, I just might turn into the dust that is often left unseen. I just don't have the strength to try anymore. What's the point in living when there's no one there to cherish your breaths or measure the rhythm of your heartbeat anyway? Carl abandoned me too many times, and over the years I guess I just got lost in the pain. One more push could be the beginning of my last fall, though, and I bet Carl will be too busy being a man to catch me on the way down. I mean, can you blame me for being such a dedicated and faithful wife? Living to please your husband shouldn't be an unusual habit. I'm yearning for the chance to wallow in the bliss of the love we once knew, and I must decide if it's worth it... if *I'm* worth it.

Crazy days are better than lazy days. That's what they tell me. But I AM NOT CRAZY. Why can't they understand that? I'm me. Sheila Yvette Henderson. Born on November 23, 1976 at 5:40 p.m. in the infant wing of University Hospital. I'm human. I breathe and bleed just like everyone else. I am no different. Strange maybe, but still regular. My condition may not be common, but I am still me, a salient sista who just wants to be loved. If Carl doesn't love me, no one will. How can I get him to change?

My daddy was a piece of shit and Mama was his servant, so I have an excuse for being stupid I guess. I've accepted my defects. They're the ones still waiting for a cure. I will shun the devil with my steadfast beliefs. Faith taught me how to keep believing without expecting to receive a stimulus package. I knew she wasn't joking when she told me God knows all and sees all. He will seldom forsake us. As long as we learn to obey His strict command, we can expect to be saved. I've been waiting for Him to throw me my life vest for the longest, but my only lifeguard must be off duty.

Wet dreams of passion
hot flashes of fear
I know he's here ... again

Carl's punches are always so sudden. The cadence and aggressive grunts during the timing of his reign of control leaves me suffocating for puffs of air. He doesn't even have to strangle me to make me lose my breath, and I am always prepared to reenact the scenes in slow motion.

Brenda

Chapter 21:
Stop Means Go

Apparently, speaking proper English is against the law for a black woman. I'm an educated sista who needs an educated brotha to help me balance out this racist world that's full of hypocrites and judgmental scouts. I can't even have a drink without feeling like they're staring me down and undressing me with their filthy imaginations. DeAngelo was cute, but he's no different from the others. All men are good for is using their magic tool to hypnotize and control a woman for thirty minutes or less. I've learned their tricks though, and no man will ever take advantage of my body without my permission again. I'm the ruler of this sex shit.

Brenda's daily struggle always seemed to get the best of her logical thinking. Trying to comprehend what happened to her so many years ago was a never-ending cycle of disappointment and pain. Although she longed for love and companionship, she enjoyed her independence and the freedom to do whatever the hell she wanted. Any man who tried to get in the way of that was in for a rude and disrespectful awakening.

"Fuck you!" Brenda yelled at the driver of each car who honked their horns at her reckless directional attempts. She rapidly passed each intolerant asshole with aggression and impatience. Drinking and driving may not be the best idea, but Brenda had become a pro at manipulating her levels of intoxication just enough to get to where she needed to go.

After many years of faithfully consuming alcoholic beverages, she had turned into a careless risk taker who has no regard for the lives of others, or even her own. Brenda got a daily kick out of swerving between vehicles on the highway and skillfully avoiding accidents, as well as nights spent behind bars from offering sexual encounters to every officer that had ever pulled her over in exchange for her freedom. So far, she had solicited her goods to three willing policemen, and she still possessed a current, valid license. Officer number four was now on her tail.

"Good evening, ma'am. Are you aware that you were going eighty-eight miles per hour in a seventy mile-per-hour zone?"

"No, sir. My apologies. I was in such a hurry that I didn't recognize the speed at which I was traveling."

Brenda batted her eyes in a flirtatious manner, but the officer failed to notice.

"License and registration, please," he said sternly. Brenda sat still in the car, contemplating her next, sneaky move.

"Ma'am, I'm tempted to let you off with a warning, but I see here that this isn't the first time you've disobeyed the law."

"Whatsoever do you mean officer?"

"My records indicate that you have previously been arrested for reckless endangerment, but never actually charged. Now, why is that?"

"Well, I have no idea. I guess I've just learned how to manipulate the system."

"Manipulate the system?"

"Yes, the system where handsome officers like you target beautiful women like me in the middle of the night because all the other real criminals are too smart for you to catch."

"Is that so, ma'am?"

"Absolutely, and pardon my frankness, but ma'am is such an informal term. Call me Brenda. Please and thank you, officer handsome."

"Are you getting fresh with me, ma'am?" The officer flashed a smile, so Brenda worked her basic charm and went about her business with another warning to add to her catalog of lawful exchanges. She was a clever coquette, and there was no doubt that she would be seeing officer handsome again.

Faith

Liltera R. Williams

Chapter 22:
Sin Is Sin

I may be a Christian, but I'm no saint. I wish everyone would stop treating me like I'm this absolute model of flawless existence. I'm simply a woman of God and I, too, make mistakes. Sure, I can recite the Bible word for word, but that doesn't mean I have no faults. When I agreed to enter the gates of marital bliss, I knew it wouldn't be all roses. This morning, I practically downgraded to the title of baby mama. God knows I tried. A separation was never in my plans, but I refuse to let my husband cause me to backslide. I held on to the thought long enough. God didn't change my mind, so I guess it's meant to be. Never thought I'd be saying goodbye to my forever. Then again, most things don't last always. God's got this. I'll be fine. I'm just worried about Savannah. How is she going to handle not having her daddy around? Is it selfish of me to put my needs first? I cannot keep dealing with my husband's inability to be faithful, while he's out there doing God knows what with God knows who. I'm stuck in the house taking care of his seed — a seed that we both produced. Even though I didn't want kids, I knew that becoming a mother would be good for me. He kept saying I was trying to trap him, but we were already married. That just makes me think he was planning to leave me someday. But when he saw how depressed I was after we killed the first baby, he wanted to make it all better. I wasn't sure if I would make it through my first trimester because I was so damaged from a previous sham imitation of love. My husband helped me heal, and then he damaged me some more. I was boring him, I guess. I forgot how to have fun. If God wasn't included, I didn't want to be involved. Being a single mother was not in my plans, and I've never been too good at being spontaneous. It's too late for me to learn now. I'm a grown woman with grown responsibilities. I don't have much time for fun. I just wanted to be happy. Was that too much to ask?

Sunni

Chapter 23:
She's All That

I don't know what else to do to get through to Sheila. Carl must be sneaking behind my back and telling her lies about me. She has never been this stubborn. I just want us to run away together and be happy, but she's always trying to bring Carl along, and I don't participate in threesomes. How am I supposed to get her to see the truth if I can't ever get her alone? She thinks I'm trying to tear them apart. I just want her to see the truth. I want her to find real love inside of herself and stop depending on a man to make her happy. Too bad I don't have any supersonic powers. That would make my job a whole lot easier.

"So, do you enjoy sleeping with my husband?" She must have been reading my mind incorrectly.

"I will not discuss my private affairs with you, Sheila."

"Oh, so now you want things to be private? What about the fact that you are always stalking me and strategizing over my every move? Do I not get the same benefits when it comes to our Siamese arrangement?"

"This discussion is over Sheila."

"No, actually, Sunni this discussion is just beginning. Tell me all about how my husband has been screwing your brains out."

"We don't screw, Sheila. We make love. Passionate love. And we don't use condoms. Is that what you want to hear?"

"You bitch!"

"No, Sheila I think you may have Brenda and me confused. I am not a bitch."

"Yes, you are! A bitch and a home wrecker. Why can't you just go back to where you came from? You're messing everything up for me."

"I'm not messing anything up, Sheila. You are finally able to see the truth and you can't handle it."

"The truth about what?"

"You know what truth I'm speaking of. There is no need to repeat what I have been telling you since the day we met."

"Just shut up!"

"You cannot silence me, Sheila. No matter how hard you try. I will always be a part of you."

"I hate you!"

"And that's the problem. If you never learn to love me, you will never be happy. I am not here to upset you. I just want you to embrace me."

"Never!"

"OK, Sheila. You obviously need more time to think things through. I'm leaving now, but I'll be back. Hopefully, next time you'll be willing to understand me a little better. I love you, even when you don't love yourself."

Sheila

Chapter 24:
No More Sunni Days

S unni doesn't want me. She just wants my husband. I can't let her take him away from me. I have to end this three-way warfare now, before it's too late for all of us.

"Sunni, I'm home!"

"Sunni doesn't live here anymore!"

"Oh shit! Sheila? Sheila, why are you bleeding?"

"I killed Sunni."

"What?"

"I killed her."

"Sheila, what do you mean you killed Sunni? You cut yourself."

"I know. Sunni is dead, so I can have my husband all to myself now."

"Sheila, you're talking crazy."

"I'm not crazy, Carl!"

"OK, I'm sorry. We need to get you to a hospital."

"No! All I need is you, Carl. Make love to me like you used to. The way you made love to Sunni."

"I can't right now, Sheila. You're bleeding. Let me take you to a hospital."

"No, you know what happened the last time you took me to a hospital. They kept me away from you for six months. I can't go through that again. I just want you to make love to me, Carl. That will make it all better."

"Sheila I can't. Please let me take you to a hospital."

"No, Carl!"

Why doesn't he want to make love to me? I am not much different than Sunni. We look the same, talk the same, and dress the same. I guess we don't sex the same. He screws me and makes love to her. Well, not anymore. She's dead now, so he has no choice but to make love to me and only me. I know just what to do to change his mind.

"Sheila, what are you doing?"

"I'm showing my husband just how much I love him." I started kissing on his neck and nibbling on his ear, just the way he likes. "Take off your shirt."

"Sheila, this is insane."

"No, this is normal. Take off your shirt like I said."

He removed it slowly and then I unbuckled his pants. He closed his eyes and relinquished all control. I kissed his lips softly. He refused to participate at first, so I used my tongue to awaken his senses, strolling it along his bottom lip and then gently biting as my need to have him inside of me was surmounting. He finally gave in and properly scooped me up and carried me to the bathroom. We slid through the doorway and he undressed me carefully. The blood had soaked my garments, but I did not mind. Even the most expensive blouse from Saks Fifth Avenue could not come between me and my husband. This was long overdue. He turned on the shower and tested the temperature. He knows I like it warm and steamy. Then, he turned to me and smiled. He hasn't smiled at me in so long. I wanted to please him so badly. I approached him seductively and began to rub on his bare skin.

"I've missed you so much, Carl."

"I've never left you, Sheila. You were the one always disappearing on me."

"I know, Carl. I'm so sorry."

"It's OK, Sheila."

"Make love to me, Carl. Show me how much you've missed me, too."

His hands smothered my breasts and he caressed my nipples with the tip of his tongue. My moans were a signal for him to continue. I gripped the back of his head and motioned for him to move in circles. His tongue hit the spot as he stretched my nipples with his teeth. It's been a while since I felt pleasure like this.

"Make love to me, Carl. Now. I need you now."

"I am making love to you, Sheila. Just relax."

"Please, Carl. I can't take it."

"Are you sure, Sheila? You're still bleeding and I don't want to hurt you."

"Yes, Carl. I am sure. Please stop stalling."

He lifted me into the shower and with the water streaming down my back I could feel him sliding all the way through me, slowly and calmly. The most calm he's ever been. He held one of my legs up and offered me long strokes with short pauses in between. It was slippery, but I felt safe in his arms. He has never made love to me like this before, taking his time to make sure that I am pleased.

"Carl?"

"Yeah?"

"This feels so good."

"I'm glad you like it."

We slipped down to the floor of the bathtub and he positioned me on top of him.

"Your turn," he said.

With my palms stuck to the tile and my breasts standing at attention in front of his face, I followed his lead, scooting up and sitting down with a slight pinch of aggression. I heard his silent cries for me to slow down as I sped up the pace, but I couldn't stop until I heard him say it.

"Tell me you love me." Silence.

I kept a steady speed, trying so hard not to release, but I knew he was about to.

"Say it. Tell me you love me." Silence again.

I turned around, without removing him from inside of me. I leaned forward and felt him squeeze my hips right before I froze.

"Please tell me you love me. I need to hear it." Another moment of silence, and then he said it.

"I love you, Sunni."

I turned back around to see his face covered in moisture. It was not the steam from the shower. Instead, tears for water, clear as day. I snatched him out of me. His penis was still hard and I was shocked. I tried to step out of the tub, but he grabbed my arm and slung me to the floor.

"Please don't go. I said I love you."

I didn't know what to say. He was crying. I had never seen Carl cry before. This was serious and I could finally step outside of myself long enough to see it. I flashed back to when I was thirteen. To the last time. The last time he touched me.

Float like a butterfly, sting like a bee ... Muhammad Ali's metaphor snuck its way into our moment and I was floating on top of his ship. He made love to me. It was more than sex. I know what sex feels like and it was the total opposite of any experience I could scramble up to even compare. It was magic. He was the magician and I was captivated by his tricks. There was no rush to get to the shore. We were coasting, slow and steady and I was floating. The sting of his penetrations numbed my senses. He was worthy of the pain and I want to ride this ship forever, even if I have to be someone else...

"I love you too, Daddy. Please take me to the hospital before I bleed to death."

Part II

Liltera R. Williams

*"Now faith is the substance of things hoped for,
the evidence of things not seen."*

—*Hebrews 11:1*

Brenda

Liltera R. Williams

Chapter 25:
No Symptoms = No Solution

irror, mirror on the wall, who's the craziest of them all? I suppose it's me. For years I have been overlooking what has always been right in front of my face. The wigs. The makeup. The outfit changes. None of it could ever cover up how dirty I've always felt on the inside. If I could turn back the hands of time, I would pray for God to transform me into someone else. I was never good at being me. Who am I, anyway? I honestly don't know. I was tossed out of my mother's womb into a dungeon that offered me no other escape, enveloped by the world's demons and cursed with hatred from those who rushed to define my character at first sight. I am a nobody and nobody cares. So, I maneuver through life, dancing to my own beat ... blending in with strangers at nightclubs and sprinting away from my sistas into the noise. I can't hear them when I'm preoccupied with my glass of scotch. It washes away the aggravation and silences their nagging, but I can still hear them when I am asleep. They're in my dreams, nightmares rather, trying to scare me straight. However, I am still the twisted bitch they've always known. I guess I'll never change.

"Brenda, I think it's time for you to get some serious help. Talking to me isn't allowing you to make much progress."

"I am fine, Dr. Sebastian."

"Fine isn't enough. If I can't get you to happy then we are wasting each other's time."

"I am happy."

"No, Brenda. You are content. Being content does not mean you are happy."

"Whatever you say, Doc."

"Why did you cut yourself this time?"

"Because Carl loves Sunni more than he loves Sheila."

"What does that have to do with you and who is Sunni?"

"I am Sunni."

"I don't get it."

"Sunni is me."

"Brenda, I don't have time for you to be foolish. You've been straightforward since we've started our sessions. Why are you sealing up your confessions now all of a sudden?"

"I'm not sealing up anything, Doc. Sunni is who I am when I am happy and not just content."

"So you've created another clone of yourself?"

"I didn't create her. She just showed up."

"When, Brenda?"

"A couple years ago. She keeps leaving and coming back. I can't remember exactly when she showed up, but it was close to the first time Carl hit Sheila."

"How did it happen?"

"How did what happen?"

"How did she show up?"

"I don't remember."

"Come on, Brenda. If you want me to help you, you have to be honest with me."

"I am being honest. I don't remember how she showed up. I just know that she doesn't like to come around when Sheila and Faith are invited."

"Who are Sheila and Faith again?"

"My sistas."

"I know you don't have any siblings, Brenda, so please help me understand."

"When Carl leaves to go looking for Sunni on Sundays, I worship with Faith, but still commit sins afterwards. God will never forgive me. I'm better off dead."

"Brenda, I am not following you."

"It's OK, Doc. You're not the first person who has called me a liar. I have to go. I only have a few more days left to spend with my husband before he sails off to go look for Sunni again."

"Brenda, wait."

"Save it, Doc. You don't ever have to worry about me coming back to see you again, either."

I knew she wouldn't understand. No one ever will. I could really use a drink right now.

Faith

Chapter 26:
She Told Me to Keep the Faith

Sheila keeps blaming Brenda for her current state of turmoil and I can't keep the peace. I've tried and I've tried again, but neither of them will budge and I'm frankly growing tired of the bickering and complaining. There's no gratefulness anywhere to be found. Brenda has always been jealous of the way Sheila skipped right along, leaving us behind to gather our senses. I'm not sure if Brenda will ever let it go and I'm not sure if Sheila will ever realize how much pain she has caused. I can't keep trying to indulge in such a draining task. I need them both to cooperate and to be open to reconciliation. Otherwise, we're all doomed to hell. God will not allow us to continue this drama in heaven, that's if we make it in.

I can barely stand to watch. How in the world did it even get to this point? I remember when Brenda would smile for no reason at all, and now she barely even flashes a grin … always angry and bitter, holding on to things that happened in the past. She has become this alcoholic mortal, sanitizing her pain with poison and Sheila is just the standby victim who rejects all sources of help. And sadly, I have become helpless in my quest to rekindle the love of my sistas. God knows. I can feel Him pulling me away from them. How can one person be so crowded, but feel so lonely … so busy yet idle? So contaminated. My sistas are polluted with sin and I have been pushed into the spotlight. But I am tempted to walk away … leave all of this secular mess behind to enjoy my blessings in peace. They don't want to be saved and I don't want to be disappointed. I know for a fact that this will not be the last time I'll have to come to their rescue, just to have them revisit the same death trap. I want to live and I want to live free of their shame. I can't let them wrap me up into their web of pity. If God knows me, then He knows that this is not something I can handle on my own. No matter how many times I try to prove what should already be evidently clear, they find a way to make me contradict my stance on the Word. I am a Christian and they are obviously not prepared to accept me as such. We can't all coexist in harmony without compromising, but I refuse to compromise with people who are not contributing to my spiritual growth. God help us all.

Liltera R. Williams

Sheila

Liltera R. Williams

Dear Lord,

My prayers have gone unanswered. Why are you taking so long to show yourself? My sistas need you and so do I. I drag them to church with me every Sunday. We pay our tithe and we even fast when the pastor tells us to. Why can't we get rewarded for our obedience sooner rather than later? I don't know how much longer Sheila is going to last with Brenda telling her what to do. Can you step in, please? Like now, meaning right now. You told us to keep the faith, but faith doesn't come with a tutorial on how to be patient. Please, God, help us now. Amen.

"Are you praying again?"

"Yes, I am."

"Why? God is obviously ignoring us."

"He isn't ignoring us, Sheila. He is simply taking His time."

"If you say so."

"I do say so. What is your problem, Sheila? Can't you see why God hasn't shown up yet? You won't let Him. Where is your faith?"

"She's standing right next to me."

"This is not a joke, Sheila. You are about to lose everything you've worked so hard for. I hope it's worth it."

"You don't know what you're talking about, Faith!"

I yelled as loud as I could, but she was already gone. Everyone is always leaving me. I guess that's what people were born to do. Leave. I've been all by myself since I was thirteen. I can handle it. I don't need Sunni, Faith, or Brenda to help me get through this. Who needs sistas anyway? I never got used to being an only child, but I know what it feels like to be alone. It sucks. It's like playing Scrabble all by yourself, waiting for someone who can't spell to make the next move. I never learned any shortcuts. I always like to do things the right way. Spur of the moment activities are like shorthand messages, hard to decipher. I am scribbling my story on a sidewalk with broken chalk, and they keep stomping on it, so I'm running out of things to say. I am stammering my way through the darkness, stuttering with each repetitive confession, and still being ignored. I told them I was afraid of the dark, but I still ended up here. So much for family first.

Liltera R. Williams

Peace on earth is nonexistent
Your love of self is far and distant
How can we get along if you refuse to talk in private
You said all that stuff about me
Still I kept quiet
They told me to turn the other cheek
But now I can't hide it
You lash out and curse,
then throw God in the mix
Don't you know He can't hear you
when you're talking in skits
You need help
Jealousy is deadly
If you really don't care
Then go ahead and dead me
Misery loves company
Stop inviting me in
Learn the Ten Commandments
Bearing false witness is a sin
They say it's just the way you are
and how you've always been
But how am I supposed to just deal with this feeling?
When someone hates you
There's no such thing as healing...

Dearly Beloved S.I.S.T.A.S

Liltera R. Williams

Chapter 27:
Seven Minutes to Seven

She was a beautiful, broken soul. Although I could not seep through the guard that shielded her pain, I knew she needed me, but I just couldn't stay. The constant rejection of my attempts to bring her joy and holding her through distant moments filled with tears and emptiness left me cold and isolated. She longed for peace within herself and I simply wanted to give her all the love I had inside of me. It wasn't enough for the both of us. I couldn't erase the scars of betrayal and abandonment. I couldn't help her become a woman of honor, a woman of dignity, a woman with no shame. She wanted to do it on her own. Her quest to conquer cowardice tendencies was a notorious expedition. I often wonder how she's doing … if she smiles when she reflects on the wonderful memories of our union … if she knows that I will always care, or if she even cares enough to remember everything I have seemed to forget...

"We are gathered here today for what, Faith?"

"Sheila has something to tell us, so please save your hostility. She needs our support."

"Well, what is it? I don't have much time to waste."

"Just be patient, will you Brenda? This is exactly why she stopped keeping us informed in the first place. You were never understanding enough."

"I was as understanding as I could be."

"Well, can you try a little harder, please? For me?"

"I guess so."

"Thank you."

"Brenda. Faith. I want y'all to meet Sunni."

"Who is Sunni?"

"The woman I love."

"The woman you love? What do you mean by that, Sheila?"

"Exactly what I said. Sunni, say hello to my sistas."

"Hello Brenda and Faith. Sheila has told me all about you two."

"Well, we've never heard anything about you."

"Brenda, please don't be rude."

"I'm not being rude. I'm being honest. So are you trying to tell us that you're gay, Sheila?"

"I don't like to call it that. I have fallen in love."

"Well what do you call it when two women fall in love with each other?"

"Freedom."

"Freedom? What do you mean freedom? What about Carl?"

"Carl doesn't have anything to do with this."

"What? Sheila, have you lost your mind? Carl is your husband. He has everything to do with it."

"Carl is not the person I am meant to be with."

"So you're walking out on your marriage with a man for another woman?"

"Faith, I wish you wouldn't address it like that."

"Well, that's what you're telling us. God would not be pleased with this, Sheila."

"And why not? Doesn't God want me to be happy? Why does it matter if it's with a man or a woman? As long as I am with someone who loves me and respects me."

"Sheila, as much as I want to jump for joy at the fact that you are considering walking out on Carl, I really don't know if I can stand by this."

"I don't need you to stand by me, Brenda. You never have anyway. I just wanted you and Faith to know the truth."

"The truth? So are you gay or not, Sheila?"

"Are you black or white, Brenda?"

"You're equating race with sexuality. It's not the same."

"You're mixing common sense with stupidity. I guess we're both confused."

"I'm not confused about anything. I know who I am."

"Do you really?"

"Yes, I do. You're the one who seems to have forgotten where you come from."

"I have not forgotten. I simply choose not to acknowledge it."

"I didn't mean to cause any tension, ladies, but Sheila and I love each other and that's all that matters."

"No offense, Sunni, but you don't know Sheila the way that we do."

"No offense to you either, Brenda, but where have you been for the last two years?"

"Obviously Sheila did not want us around and I guess you're the reason."

"I suppose so."

"Can we all just pray about this?"

"No, Faith. It's too late for that. God can't change my mind. Sunni and I are running away together and I just wanted to tell you and Brenda goodbye … for good."

"Goodbye?"

"What do you mean goodbye, Sheila? We're your sistas. You can't tell us goodbye. Not now. Not ever."

"I'm sorry, Faith, but it's just time for me to move on."

"Move on? You make it sound as though Brenda and I mean nothing to you."

"It's not like that, Faith. I just need to start over."

"How many fucking times are you going to start over Sheila?"

"This is my fucking decision, Brenda, whether you like it or not. Just crawl back into your space and go on living your life like you always do. You're entitled to freedom, but I can't have it? Now that's not fair is it?"

"Life has never been fair for either of us, Sheila, but that doesn't mean you can just walk out. Your problems won't disappear just because you do."

"Faith, I appreciate your concern, but it's no longer needed. I'll always love you and Brenda, but I love Sunni more. I'm sorry. I'm sure God will make you forgive me someday."

"Sheila wait."

"No, Faith, just let her go."

"I can't just let her go. She needs us."

"Maybe she doesn't anymore."

"I will not accept this, Sheila! What God has for you is for you and you need to stop running!"

Sheila was already gone and Sunni had left right along with her. Once again, Sheila was preparing for another fresh start. This time, it would be without her husband. She would always appreciate the life she shared with Carl, of course before the bad began to outweigh the good, but Sunni loved her more and the love that Sunni offered was pure, and it never hurt. That's what Sheila needed. She gave her life with Carl one last acknowledgment, and then she prepared herself for the next step.

When Carl came along, I had halfway removed the recollection of my past from the deepest sections that filled the capacity of my mind. I was controlled by a burning desire to feel wanted. Carl knew just what to do and I was eager to satisfy his pursuit. Immediately infatuated with the cat and mouse chase, I quickly declared "yes" to his inquiry of a first date. I was ready to be committed. No man had ever penetrated my sacredness, except for Daddy. Carl kept telling me that he was too afraid of infecting me with his curse of neglect. I wanted him to be the one to break me in, wear me down, and build me back up again, and I was sure that he would not disappoint.

He gave me seventy-seven kisses when it was seven minutes to seven and didn't stop until seven minutes later. He told me my skin was so smooth and my lips were soft. He seduced me with conversation and a listening ear — a sweet combination of bliss. I had never felt anything like it. For some reason I felt sure — sure that he wouldn't hurt me, suddenly desert me or secretly be discreet because he opened up his world to me and allowed me to seep my way in. That grin that I've been longing to study for seconds at a time made me lose my mind, but at this point I've climaxed enough to make straight A's. I've been thinking about him for the past seven days and for the next seven months or seven years I will disobey my fears. I don't see a problem with giving him my undivided attention. I almost forgot to mention that he also cooks. I ignored his abnormal looks and absorbed him as a creative crook. He's usually not the physical type that I fall for, but this time the scenery was different. He offered me an imprint and exposed his past ... gave me the option of deciding if I wanted it to last. He was so damn gentle. He steadily caressed my mental and made me orgasm before he even touched the physical aspects of my existence. He stroked me deep, to the beat of our very own sapiosexual seclusion. I was not ready for this type of unexpected intrusion, but I came anyway. When he asked me to stay the night, I knew that it wouldn't be right to say no. He has vividly supplied me with an answer to the question I have been seeking so much to know and define. Where do broken hearts go? Whitney Houston's sad line. They are trapped in time until someone comes along looking to find their sole one. It's as if she was searching for more than what she was born to be. Much like me, but this Superman swiftly dropped in to successfully set me free, and I've been flying ever since. His innocence is intriguing. He tickles me with his teasing and makes my heart feel like it is secure for the time being, as well as the first time ever. He's waiting for the one who can make him better and I believe that I am her. I have already saved and stored his deep, dark facts. All he wants is a woman who will scratch his back and rub his head when he is thinking. Someone who will scream "what's on your mind right now?" when he's staring into space and daydreaming. A Superwoman to savor all that he offers to last. Someone who will understand and accept the struggles of his vast experiences. A down ass chick instead of a loud ass bitch. He wants something sacred and I've been saving all my love for someone like him to steal and take it. I'm not scared that he will break it in two, because his half plus my half is seven times the lucky proof that truth does still exist. I will forever long for a kiss like the one that he gave me. I was soaked in my wetness before he even grazed me. He has made me believe in love at first sight again. When we automatically anticipate that something will be sour at first bite, that's the world's highest sin. His intelligence is an exclusive entity, and even if our moment of serendipity was actually the facade of an experimental case, I'll cherish the moment he looked at me in the face and called me gorgeous. I became his darling before the sun even shined. He helped me cross the line to see all the signs of simple. He thinks his right cheek with the dimple serves as a scar of imperfection. However, he has shifted me into a pure direction, presenting a synonymous meaning for that too-good-to-be-true confession. He's too good to be alone.

I was waiting for something ... something that starts with an S, and I think I have finally been introduced to my soul mate.

Our first night of passion led to seven married years of misery. I've been begging him to offer me a seat inside his secret place of solitude. I can tell that he always feels safe when he escapes to indulge in his thoughts. I no longer want to be stuck in a battle of unwarranted abuse, fighting for my life and hoping that he will stop putting me in danger and be the one who saves me.

I wonder if he knows how much I was willing to sacrifice for his love. Cold evenings are always soothing. If only I could freeze the breeze and trap the chill of winter's blessings to cover this burning fire of anger every time it sneaks up on me. The scorch of Carl's violent fists didn't allow me to sew through these moments for long. So I cuddle with frozen memories and enjoy the heat of the night as often as I can. It sparkles when he's not around. I guess that means I'm getting closer to my breakthrough. I never imagined life without him, but Sunni has promised to take me to a place that would be nothing like my past. I trust her and I am ready.

Part III

Sheila

Chapter 28:
Solitary Confinement

"Sheila Henderson?"

"Yes, that's my wife. Can I see her?"

"No, sir. I'm sorry. No visitors allowed. She needs to rest."

"I need to see her. Please. I need to know that she is OK."

"I can assure you that she is fine, sir. You don't look very well, though. Is there something that we can do to help you get through this?"

"No. I'm fine. I just need to see my wife."

"Once again, sir, I am sorry. No visitors allowed."

"I understand."

"Good, but you should really get checked out. That rash on your skin needs to be treated. How long have you had it?"

"About a week now."

"Let me see if I can get you seen. Do you have any identification with you?"

"Yes. My name is Carl Henderson. Here's my driver's license."

"Wonderful. Please have a seat and I will schedule you a STAT appointment. Don't worry, sir. Your wife will be just fine. You have to be strong enough to be there for her when she's released."

"Yeah. Thanks."

Winter isn't always cold, but summer usually burns like hell. His fiery fists shined way brighter than the sun, and I elevated to the highest degree of inflamed misunderstanding. My soul is damaged ... crushed to pieces. Because he was too busy looking for something inside of me — something that I always failed to see. I couldn't control the climate of his temper. I just wished he would learn to practice being calm more often, like the leaves in fall, the way they blow in the gentle wind. But Carl didn't know the meaning of gentle, and practice didn't make perfect in his case. He must hate me. They say love is a two-way street, but I've been driving down this one-way path to misery for way too long. The flashbacks of that tragic day don't help me at all.

"Mommy, where are we going?"

"Shhh, Savannah. Just get in the car and be quiet."

"Is Daddy coming with us?"

"No, Savannah. Just hush, please. I'll explain everything to you when we get to where we're going. Right now I just need you to be very quiet, OK."

"But why, Mommy?"

"Enough with all the questions, Savannah ... just shut up! Please!"

That was the first time Sheila had ever snapped at her. Savannah's eyes watered and as Sheila attempted to apologize and comfort her, she couldn't believe the words that came out of her mouth.

"I want Sunni."

"What did you just say?"

"I said I want Sunni!"

Savannah then began to call for her, chanting her name at the top of her lungs, as if she was cheering for her favorite sports team.

"Sun-ni! Sun-ni! Sun-ni!"

Sheila was outraged. She started the car and drove off suddenly with no direction. Her mind wasn't clear.

It was flooded with thoughts of all that she had endured, from her torn marriage to her medical condition and dealing with a daughter that didn't even know who she really was. It already felt like her life was over. Savannah was still in the backseat yelling out Sunni's name. Sheila turned around to look at her. Savannah's face was flooded with tears and Sheila knew that she had to give her Sunni. It was the only way to save both of them. Sheila had her mind made up, but when she turned back around to focus on the road she realized that she had veered into another lane. She didn't have enough time to regain control of the wheel. As she was swerving left and right trying to avoid the head-on collision, she heard Savannah scream and then she blacked out.

"Mr. Henderson. The doctor is ready to see you now."

"Hello, Mr. Henderson. I'm Dr. Joseph. The nurse tells me you have some sort of rash on your hands."

"Yeah."

"You've had it for about a week now, correct?"

"Yeah. I think so."

"Let me check your vitals to see if everything else is normal."

"Not much is normal in my life anymore."

"Excuse me?"

"Nothing."

"Are you able to provide a urine sample? That's the quickest way for us to find out what's wrong."

"Yeah. I've been pissing every five minutes since last Sunday."

"Well, the nurse will be in to lead you to the restroom. I'll be back afterwards."

"Right this way, Mr. Henderson. There's a cup on the back of the toilet. Write your first and last name on it and place your sample inside the revolving door. Be sure to clean your private area with the wipe before letting your sample flow into the cup."

"Got it."

"I'll meet you in the hallway when you're done."

This is ridiculous. They're worrying about me and all I care about is Sheila. Of course they're going to tell me she's fine. It's their job to keep everyone from panicking. I know she must be lonely in there without me. I just want to tell her one thing. *I love you.* That's it. If I can just lay my eyes on her for a second, then I will be satisfied. Dammit! What have I done? If it wasn't for me, she probably wouldn't even be in here. I am such a fool. They say once a good woman goes bad she's gone forever. I've lost her and Sunni, and it's all my fault.

"Mr. Henderson. Are you OK in there?"

"Uhhh. Yeah. Coming out now."

"Your room is straight down the hall, first door on the left. I'm going to test your sample and Dr. Joseph will be back in to consult with you shortly."

"Thanks."

"No problem."

There's nothing wrong with me. I'm just paranoid because of what I've done to Sheila. I guess it's my turn to suffer. I'll take all the blame. I'll deal with it like a man, as long as I know that Sheila will be OK.

"Mr. Henderson?"

"Yeah, come on in."

"First of all, before I give you the results, tell me how you're feeling."

"Incomplete."

"That's understandable. Well, the good news is you're not HIV positive, but you do have symptoms of another type of sexually transmitted disease. We'll have to do some blood work and run a few more tests. This may take a few hours. Are you able to spend the night?"

Sexually transmitted disease? Carl was alarmed, but more worried about Sheila.

"I guess so. It's not like my wife is waiting for me at home."

"I understand, sir."

"No, I don't think you do. I need to see her."

"Sir, I believe more than one of our staff members has told you that we don't allow visitors in the psych ward. Your wife needs time to heal. Any type of distraction may cause her to relapse."

"Even a visit from her husband? She needs to know that I am here."

"I'll tell you what. I can have her psychologist come down to meet with you to give you an update on her condition. Will that help?"

"I guess that's better than nothing."

"Good. I will see what I can do."

"Thanks."

"First, let me take your blood and have it sent to the lab."

At least they're trying to understand. I'm driving myself crazy worrying about Sheila. I should have never made love to her while she was bleeding. I should have just taken her straight to the hospital.

"Mr. Henderson?"

"It's open."

"Hello, Mr. Henderson. I'm Dr. Sebastian, your wife's psychologist."

"Hello, Dr. Sebastian. How is she?"

"She's fine, but it's hard for us to diagnose her condition."

"What condition?"

"You haven't noticed how strange she's been acting lately?"

"Yes, I have, but she's been that way since we've met. I just learned to adjust."

"Really? Has she ever gotten any help before?"

"Yes, a few times, but the doctors always said there was nothing they could do. They just gave her a bunch of medication and she stopped taking it."

"When did she stop taking it?"

"I don't know."

"Well, Mr. Henderson, we can't help your wife if you are not willing to do all that you can to supervise her when we are not around."

"How am I supposed to supervise a grown woman?"

"By caring for her, listening to her, being patient with her, and holding her when she needs you to."

"I do all of that."

"Do you, Mr. Henderson? From what she has told me, you two haven't been getting along for the past two years."

"What did she tell you?"

"She says you've been cheating on her. That you leave her alone every Sunday to go looking for a woman named Sunni."

"So you know about Sunni?"

"Yes, I do, but I am too confused to even provide a clear synopsis on the situation. Can you fill me in?"

"Sheila is Sunni. Sunni shows up when she is severely depressed. On Sundays, when she goes to church, she usually comes back happy, and I take advantage of her when she's happy."

"Who is Brenda?"

"I have no idea who Brenda is. I've never met her."

"Hmmm ... well, I have been holding sessions with Brenda every Tuesday since she was thirteen. How long have you known Sheila?"

"We've been married for seven years."

"And she's never mentioned Brenda?"

"No. Not at all."

"This sounds like a common condition — a condition that I was afraid of."

"What is it?"

"I can't say until I am absolutely positive. I don't want to misdiagnose her. What else can you tell me?"

"About what?"

"About your wife."

"I miss her."

"I'm sure you do."

"I love her."

"Does she know how much you love her?"

"I hope so."

"When is the last time you told her?"

"Before I brought her here."

"Are you sure about that, Mr. Henderson? I'm expecting you to be totally honest with me. Your wife has told me more than I have desired to know, and I cannot help her until I know everything."

"What do you want me to say?"

"Tell me about the abuse."

"What abuse?"

"Mr. Henderson. I know all about the way you've been abusing your wife. Once, again, she has told me everything, and I need you to confirm the facts so that I am able to successfully help her."

"I didn't mean to hit her the first time."

"When was the first time?"

"Valentine's Day 2006. Our wedding night."

"Tell me what happened."

"She called me Daddy."

"In a sexual way?"

"No. I was making love to her passionately. The way I always do, and I guess it must have triggered her memory."

"Triggered her memory about her father?"

"Yes. I'm sure she's told you all about that bastard, too."

"Yes, she has. What can you tell me about him?"

"I never got the chance to meet him. From what Sheila has told me, he's dead, but if he isn't, I'll kill him myself."

"Mr. Henderson, I cannot have you talk that way in my presence."

"Sorry. I just don't understand how a man can sexually abuse his own daughter. When she first told me, I couldn't believe it, but I knew that I had to be there for her."

"Was it hard for you?"

"Yes, very much so."

"How did you handle it?"

"By hitting her."

"Why did you hit her?"

"Because I knew it would make her forget, and I didn't want her to compare me to him. I'm nothing like him!"

"I understand, Mr. Henderson, but it seems as though hitting her has only made her condition worse. She can hardly remember anything now."

"Does she remember me?"

"I can't say for sure. Her discoveries are revealed in spurts."

"I don't want her to forget me. I'm sorry."

"I know you are, Mr. Henderson. Your wife has been dealing with some serious issues all her life. You should not have tried to save her all by yourself."

"But she kept telling me that I was all she needed."

"That's common. Most patients dealing with a mental issue are stuck in denial for years. They think everyone wants to harm them."

"I didn't hurt her on purpose. I was only trying to help."

"Mr. Henderson, it appears as though you need help as well. Your wife's condition has caused you to overlook the reality of things. That is evident in your addressing her as Sunni instead of Sheila, without hesitation. She has warped you into thinking that she is somebody else."

"I am not warped."

"Indeed you are, Mr. Henderson. We are doing all that we can to help your wife, but you also need our help."

"I'm not crazy."

"I didn't say that you were. I simply said you need help."

"No, I need my wife."

"Your wife is unavailable for the next six weeks. How will you cope to pass the time?"

"I don't know."

"Do you smoke?"

"No, I don't smoke. What kind of question is that?"

"A normal one. I am attempting to gather a rundown of how you handle stress."

"I'm a lawyer. I'm familiar with stressful situations."

"Good. How do you handle them?"

"By studying, mostly."

"Studying what?"

"Law books. The Bible."

"So would you consider yourself to be a religious person?"

"Of course. I believe in God."

"Good. There's a Bible in the top drawer. Study it. I'll be back with more information for you in the morning."

Chapter 29:
Sorry Again

He'll probably never forgive me for giving him an STD. I can't keep my eyes closed long enough to replay the scenes of every other man I was sleeping with. Carl was always by biggest supporter. That's why I tried so hard to always be Sunni when he needed me to be. I just couldn't unfasten the shackles. They kept locking me up and trying to make me be Sheila when all that I ever wanted to be was a strong, intelligent, sassy sista with high self-esteem. They would never loosen the strain of my resistance. Instead, they stuffed seeds of destruction down my throat and tried to forcefully heal me from my squared mentality, while stretching me at the four corners that steadily connected me and gave me the balance I needed to stand.

What are you really supposed to do to make them realize that you are not skewed to the point of no return? I was eventually coming back, but I had to give Sunni enough time to synchronize the dots and seal us all back together again. They kept trying to shut me up when I was shouting, and they were always too distracted to fully analyze the significance of each SOS that seeped into the steamed air from each breath I struggled to catch. What else could I do to cry out for help? I was hardly ever Sunni long enough to suppress the darkness before day came. I wonder if they will look close enough to understand me now that Sunni is lost. They just don't understand me. How can I prove to them that I'm not crazy if they keep ignoring me? Hello! Can anybody hear me?

"I hear you, Sheila. Stop yelling so loud before they kick you out."

"That's what I want them to do, Sunni."

"You need more time. Last time you were here, it didn't work. Let them do their job, Sheila."

"I am not some experiment, Sunni. They shouldn't keep performing observational surgery on me when there is absolutely nothing wrong."

"That's the problem, Sheila. You won't admit that there is something wrong with you. Stop fighting it. The sooner you accept it, the better things will be."

"Why are you always on their side, Sunni?"

"Because I need some fresh air. Being stuck in here with you is beginning to drive me crazy as well."

"That's not funny."

"And I'm not laughing. Sheila, how many times do I have to tell you that life is about choices? When you make the right choices everyone ends up happy in the end."

"Well, what choice am I supposed to make?"

"You know the answer to that question, Sheila. Just let me know when it's time to go."

Carl was so worried about Sheila. He knew that he had contributed to her breakdown, but there was nothing that he could do at this point to make up for it.

"Mr. Henderson, when is the last time you had intercourse?"

"Last Sunday. Why?"

"With whom?"

"Sunni ... I mean Sheila."

"Mr. Henderson, we need to know exactly who you've been intimate with. That person may need to be tested as well."

"Tested for what?"

"I'd rather not say just yet until we know for sure, but you must not be sexually active for about six weeks. That shouldn't be hard since your wife isn't scheduled to be released until then."

"Tell me what's wrong with me, Doc."

"I will ... when the time is right. For now, we need you to get some rest. Try not to worry about your wife so much. Once again, she will be fine."

Faith

Chapter 30:
We Clap Our Hands in the Sanctuary

"But they that wait upon the LORD shall renew their strength; they shall mount up with wings as eagles; they shall run, and not be weary; and they shall walk, and not faint." —Isaiah 40:31

God said be patient. He didn't say be perfect. That's my problem. I've always tried to be perfect. Every little thing always has to be on point. I just want to learn how to live on impulse … how to worry less and be fine with things being out of order. I want to walk out of the house and be OK with forgetting my Bible, because God knows the type of life I desire to lead. I am always living to please Him, and that's all that matters. For once, I just want everyone to stop depending on me to be good. I make mistakes. I am human. No matter how hard I try to be controlled by the Holy Spirit, I will falter, and God understands. I can't change the fact that people don't. I have yet to learn that I cannot please people. Even though I have surpassed them spiritually, I am still a vessel of the world. There is so much going wrong in my life, but as long as I focus on the right, I will be just fine.

"Sheila, if you're listening to me, God told me to tell you that He has not forsaken you."

"Well, what's taking Him so long to show up, Faith? How much more can I endure in this secluded sanctuary?"

"Sheila, I've told you countless times that God wants you to trust Him and you keep letting it go in one ear and out the other. I will not keep repeating myself if you're too stubborn to obey His command."

"Why should I keep believing, Faith? I'm stuck and obviously God doesn't even know how to get to me. Where's Carl? How is he doing?"

"Carl is fine, Sheila. Brenda stopped by to check on him last week."

"You know I don't want that slut around my husband! Faith, please make sure they are never alone again. She can't be trusted."

"OK, Sheila. I will do that, but you have to promise me that you will not lose hope. We need you to be strong."

"Faith, I wish I could make you that promise, but I just don't know if I am able to take a walk in someone else's shoes right this second. My sentences are shortening now. Talk to you soon."

"I sure hope so."

Sheila

Liltera R. Williams

Chapter 31:
Not-So-Angry Black Sista

I hate him. But I love him even more. He doesn't mean to hurt me. I know it. He just gets a little out of control sometimes. I have to learn how to be more understanding and stop pissing him off so much. I know what I'll do. I'll cook his favorite dish for dinner when I get out of here — spaghetti with meatballs and cheese sprinkled on top. Maybe we'll make love again. I just hope the next time he'll be able to see me as Sheila instead of Sunni. I wish she would just go back to where she came from. Ever since she showed up, she has caused me nothing but trouble. She stole my husband and my family. No one needs me. I would rather feel alone than unwelcomed.

I still remember the day I told Carl I was pregnant again. I had finally built up the courage to stand up to him, but for the thirteenth time, he knocked me down with a strike to the stomach. I thought that it would surely make me lose baby number two. He made me abort the first one because he didn't think that I was fit to be a mother, and he didn't want to end up as a single father. It was a girl and I named her Savannah. She had my nose and Carl's eyes. I wonder what she would look like if she were alive today. She would have been ten years old this year.

"Carl, guess what?"
"What?"
"I'm pregnant!"
"From who?"
"You, Carl."
"I don't think so."
"What do you mean you don't think so?"
"We can't have a baby, Sheila."
"Why not?"
"You know why not. How far along are you?"
"I don't know. About four weeks I guess."
"Good. It's not too late to get rid of it."
"Get rid of it? Carl, I am not killing another baby."
"You won't be killing anything. It's not even a baby yet."
"Carl, I cannot believe you are saying this to me."

"Well, believe it, Sheila. I need more time to build my law firm."

"How can you be so selfish?"

"I am not being selfish, Sheila. I am being smart."

"Is that what you call it? Well, that is the stupidest thing I've ever heard."

"You better watch your tone when you're talking to me, woman."

"Why, Carl? Why do you get to make all of the decisions in this marriage?"

"Watch it, Sheila."

"I am keeping this baby, and you are going to deal with it."

"Yeah, we'll see about that."

He approached me with such vengeance, staring at me with evil eyes. This time, I was prepared to fight back because I knew I was protecting someone other than myself.

"How do I know if this baby is mine? We don't even have sex that much. Who have you been sleeping with, Sheila?"

"Nobody but you, Carl. I'm not a hoe!"

"Prove it!"

"How am I supposed to prove it?"

"I want a DNA test as soon as this baby is born. If you're lying, I will kill you."

He delivered a full force blow to my face and I fell to the floor. My tears waxed the tile so often. It never lost its shine.

I still remember the first poem I wrote for Savannah. I couldn't wait for her to grow up and read it. I would give anything to be with her right now. Sometimes I can still hear her crying out for me, the same way I always cried out for Mama when Daddy wouldn't leave me alone.

Dearly Beloved S.I.S.T.A.S

Dear Little girl lonely, lost and confused
Little girl mistreated, neglected, abused
Little girl you're pretty
Little girl you're a gem
Little girl you're so much better than him
Little girl you're talented
Little girl you're smart
Little girl you're God's child
Protect your heart
Little girl slow down
Enjoy being small
Because little girl when you're older
You'll stumble and fall

Little girl don't worry
Life is all about change
Little girl things won't always be the same
Little girl you're a lady
Little girl you're loved
Little girl remember to never give up

Chapter 32:
Shhh... They Can Hear Us

Sheila, Brenda, and Faith were more than just three peas in a pod. They were sistas sharing happy memories and tragedies, and leaning on each other for support through the good, the bad, and the ugly. Now, things had gotten really ugly. Brenda's betrayal had deeply scarred Sheila and Faith was still stuck in the middle. If they're all struggling with managing their own secrets, how can they even manage to rebuild a friendship that's been torn by lies and deceit? Faith is always preaching about forgiveness.

But how am I supposed to forgive when it hurts this bad? Sheila just didn't know how.

You don't expect your sistas to be the ones to stab you in the back and then dig the knife in even deeper to do more damage. What if God was one of us? Would He truly understand how hard it is to live Holy? I'm tired of arguing about the same things, going back and forth about who's right and who's wrong. I just want us all to be happy.

"Brenda."

"Sheila."

"What are you doing here?"

"Don't ask me stupid questions."

"Whatever."

"You know exactly what I'm doing here."

"Well, I sure as hell didn't invite you."

"That's absolutely clear."

"I don't have time to argue with you. We've been through this way too many times. I'm tired of it. I know Faith is tired of it, too."

"So what do you suppose I should do?"

"You can start by getting out of my face."

"That won't happen."

"You're the enemy."

"Likewise."

"Look, Sheila, just tell me what you want so we can stop pretending to like each other for the sake of Faith's purpose."

"I want you to forgive yourself and then stop hiding."

"Hiding from what?"

"Your past, Brenda. You think changing your name and your appearance will make it all go away? It won't."

"Shut up, Sheila."

"Why? You finally need to hear the truth. I'm trapped because of you, Brenda ... because you keep running. You're running so fast that I can't keep up. God wants to save us and He can't save us if we're not on one accord. Slow down and stop running, Brenda."

"Now you're starting to sound like Faith."

"Good. You always listen to Faith. Now listen to me. It's time to change, Brenda. We can't keep going on like this. You're stunting our growth. Why are you still hiding?"

"I'm not hiding from anything."

"Yes you are, Brenda. Just face it."

"Face it? You want me to face it?"

"Yes!"

"How can I face the fact that my daddy was a drunken bastard who treated me like sloppy seconds when my mother was too busy sulking in her misery? She avoided the scrutiny and instead of allowing it to develop into a big scandal, I changed my name to escape from her slander. I'm no longer who I used to be. She can't belittle me with her alliterated insults anymore. I had to run, Sheila. You know why I'm hiding. Why must I confess to the obvious?"

"Because it's time for a change. The power of death is in the tongue, Brenda and you keep speaking nothing but negative things over our lives. Do you want us to die?"

"What do I have to live for?"

"Me!"

"Fuck you, Sheila!"

"I will not stay here to be degraded by you. I have done nothing to deserve this ... nothing but love you and deal with your obscenities from day one. You need some serious help, my sista!"

"Touché."

"I'm done with this conversation."

"Good riddance."

"I hope you'll soon grow out of this slump and learn to skip over the urge to go mad. The devil is busy, Brenda. You need to find your rest in God like Faith keeps telling us."

"God is invisible."

"And you're impossible."

"Aren't we all?"

"Have some standards, Brenda."

"Have some fun, Sheila. You're always so worried about what people think of me and you. You need to learn how to store their opinions in a big ass shack and walk away without turning around to see if they survive. People are going to judge you regardless of what you do. Stop being so damn stuck up and live. That's all I'm trying to do. Just live."

"Live how? How can I live as carefree as you when I have responsibilities? I have a daughter who depends on me to take care of her and I can't even spend time with her when I want to because there's so much shit going on in my head. She deserves to have someone who is not too busy to stop and sniff the roses in spring or watch her play in the daytime. So don't tell me to live a little when I have to live smart enough for the both of us."

"Daughter? Sheila, Savannah is no longer here."

"Stop it, Brenda. Just stop! You don't know what you're talking about."

"Sheila, you just don't get it."

"Get what? You've signed, sealed and delivered yourself to hell, and I am not letting you take me with you. Get out of my face, Brenda!"

She always does this — tries to act like she knows everything. She's the last person I should be listening to. She won't even face her own problems. How can she tell me how to deal with what I'm going through? I am perfectly fine. I don't need her or her biased opinions. Why can't they see that I am just trying to protect myself? All they want to do is hurt me. I've been hurt too many times. When will I get a chance to truly be happy? I just want to fly away from this place and never come back.

Liltera R. Williams

Brenda

Chapter 33:
All Satires Weren't Meant to be Sarcastic

L ife is too exciting to be living in fear. After all the pain I have experienced I've got the right to have some fun. I don't care what Sheila says. She's just mad because she can't live like me. I do what I want when I want. Twenty-four seven. I control me. She's always so worried about what Carl is going to think. I don't have time to be living my life for any man. Not even if he's screwing me to his maximum potential. No penis is that damn good. I keep trying to tell her that Carl is not worth it. Any man who wants to change you needs to be sent straight to hell. If he can't love you for who you are, then suspend his ass. Sheila never listens to me anyway. My advice means nothing to her. Faith always gets the final word, and they both keep telling me that I'm the one who needs to change. Why me? Why am I being singled out? Time is money, but dreaming is free. I'm running out of time, and there's no sense in dreaming when reality is going to eventually hit you. I need to find someone who can pay for me to get out of here.

"You're a trip, Brenda … a trip with no luggage and a bitter bag lady with too much to carry. When are you going to drop the dead weight?"

"The only dead weight that I'm carrying around is you, Sheila. When are you going to drop dead?"

"Why do you insist on being so disrespectful toward me?"

"You call it disrespect. I call it tough love."

"Whatever it is, it hurts, Brenda, and I'm tired of being the main target."

"Well suck it up, Sheila. You're either for me or against me and lately you haven't been acting like you don't care very much."

"What are you talking about?"

"Don't be so naïve, Sheila."

"Naïve about what?"

"Just forget it."

"No, I will not just forget it. You can't call me out on something and then renege. Tell me, Brenda. Tell me, what have I done that has you acting so selfish?"

"No matter what I tell you, it's not going to change."

"You don't know that."

"Sheila, I know you."

"Whatever, Brenda."

"You know what, Sheila, if sorry is what you want to hear then I'm sorry."

"Sorry for what?"

"For always making you feel like you're to blame. I'm the one who needs to wake up. Alcohol is only strong enough to keep me awake through the nightmares. I'm tired of being afraid."

"What is it that you're so afraid of, Brenda?"

"My past."

"Me too."

"Your past isn't as soiled as mine is, Sheila."

"You've never even asked me about it."

"That's because I already know about it. Faith told me everything."

"Well, it still would have been nice to talk to you about it. Maybe it would have helped us understand each other a lot better."

"Have we met? My name is Brenda. I specialize in sexcapades. Sausages are my favorite type of meat."

"You need help."

"No, I need Sam. He hasn't called me back since last Saturday. Have you seen him?"

"How long are you going to play this silly game, Brenda?"

"What game?"

"The game where you avoid the reality of your situation. You are addicted to sex."

"I am not addicted to sex."

"I would never sully your smartness with seeds of doubt."

"Say what?"

"You are a slave to the penis and you can't help but to enjoy the thrill."

"Why are you always talking in poetic riddles? Speak English, Sheila."

"Brenda, I am speaking as clearly as I know how. You just refuse to listen."

"I don't have time for this."

"Exactly."

"Fine, Sheila. What do you want to know?"

"I'm not saying anything else until I know you're ready to be serious."

"Ready."

"I'm not kidding, Brenda."

"Neither am I. Shoot."

"Why are you such a bitch to me?"

"Because everyone loves you and hates me."

"That is not true, Brenda."

"Yes, it is, and you know it."

"Faith loves you."

"Yeah, but what about you, Sheila? Do you love me?"

"I love you when you're not drinking and when you're not screwing every man walking."

"See. There is always a stipulation when it comes to loving me. Why can't people just accept me for who I am?"

"Because you try so hard to hide who you really are."

"I do not."

"Yes you do, Brenda. You're a specialist when it comes to keeping secrets."

"Well, it's only because I have to."

"What do you mean you have to?"

"As soon as I tell people about my past, they start treating me differently. They look beyond who I am inside and immediately begin to judge me based on my appearance."

"It's because of the way you carry yourself."

"What's wrong with the way I carry myself? Sheila, you are becoming just like them. That's why it's so hard for me to communicate with you."

"But you've never been good at communicating with anyone. Every time Faith and I tried to offer our friendship services, you still reverted back to your social tendencies."

"So?"

"As your sistas, we are supposed to always tell you the truth."

"The truth about what?"

"Brenda it is time for you to take a stance against your bad habits."

"You're my bad habit."

"That is always your response when you don't want to hear what I have to say."

"Whatever. I need a drink."

"You always need a drink. When are you going to stop drowning in your problems and start facing them?"

"When I feel like it. I'm tired of everybody telling me what I should do. Just get me out of here and let me live!"

They were at it again. Sheila and Brenda just couldn't remain cordial, and no matter how hard Faith tried to keep the peace, she knew that her sistas needed some serious help to act civilized. She prayed a prayer of forgiveness on their behalf every day, but this time her prayer was urgent. She closed her eyes and began to mumble to herself:

Dear God,

Please take away the anger and the frustrations that are affecting my sistas in those evil moments. Free their hearts, Lord, and let us all learn how to love each other again.

Amen.

Faith ended her prayer and screamed, "Stop it! Just stop it!" She knew that God would remain on call much longer than the last time, but Faith wasn't going to give up on her sistas. Not yet. They needed her now more than ever.

Sheila

Liltera R. Williams

Chapter 34:
Say What You Need to Say

There has to be more to life than this, Sheila thought. She was killing herself and everyone who tried to love her. She's always talking about those happy moments that everyone else has the pleasure of experiencing, and she always dreamed of being a character on Family Matters; a replica of Laura Winslow, minus the naivety, with Steve Urkel following her on a sandler chase before he transitioned into Stefan.

Sheila had been through enough drama in her life to generate a plethora of information for one full season. She was always known as a *goody two shoes*, even though she enjoyed walking on the wild side, but she was finally getting tired of walking alone. Sheila wants someone who cares enough to pick her up when her feet get tired and listen to her complain without placing judgment or making her feel crazier than she already knows she is … someone who will love her past her faults and dedicate themselves to helping her correct them. She has always been the stubborn one, dismissing those who try to share a piece of their happiness, and too caught up in her own mess to even think about letting someone sweep an ounce of luck under her already crowded rug. No one will ever understand just how deep her scars are. Disappearing helps her avoid the flashbacks of the arguing and the abuse, but she is finally starting to remember it all...

Mama was so desperate for a spouse that she practically begged Daddy to marry her. She gave him an ultimatum, and told him that if he didn't put a ring on it, then he would have to leave. I guess he didn't have anywhere else to go because he eventually gave her what she wanted — a stationary love; the kind of love that hardly ever sprouts. He was sworn into a commitment because Mama didn't want to be alone with me. It was the perfect scheme, and she knew how to be a shepherd, although Daddy didn't waste much time counting sheep. He was like Speedy Gonzales — hardly ever home and always on the go. I caught Mama crying a few times, but she pretended like her tears were staged. She always tried to be so strong for me. I knew she needed my shoulder to cry on, but I became selfish. I confessed my sins on paper, and gave God permission to scratch out all the errors. I wanted to learn how to forgive — how to forgive Mama for neglecting me and Daddy for cutting me with his sword, but the damage was already done. I spent so many nights locked in my room, singing sad songs with my headphones on. I knew they could hear me, but they would never interrupt, no matter how bad I wanted them to. I wanted Mama to come in and ask me what was wrong. I wanted to finally have a chance to tell her what Daddy was doing to me, but she never took the time to listen. Work consumed her, and she eventually became a superior force in our household. Daddy lost his job and started spending more time at home. When I arrived from school, he made me cater to him like a maid. I became his slore, and learned to specialize in putting other people's needs before mine. No sidebars were necessary. I thought keeping my head pointed toward the sky would keep people from butting into my business. Always smile. Be happy. That's what Mama told me. But I knew she wasn't happy, so I couldn't be either.

There were no sizable measurements for the weight I was supporting. Things got so heavy. I smuggled so much pain into my notebooks, but eventually ripped most of my poems to shreds because I knew they would hurt her feelings. And Daddy's, too. No matter what he did to me, I still loved him. I was a synthetic sapphire — a crystal so clear that you could scout me on any site. Daddy was a flammable ruby stone. Every time he got close to me, I became a girl on fire. I was never taught how to use an extinguisher, so his flames burned like hell. His anger was similar to a shockwave, with solitons spiraling all over the place. I was never good at drawing perfect shapes, but our triangle was beginning to look a lot like a sphere, and I took trips to outer space quite often.

Chapter 35:
Daddy's Sorry Letter

Dear Daddy,
Mama told me that you're still alive. If you are, then I hope you will get a chance to read this letter. I just want you to know that I'm sorry and I forgive you. I haven't seen you since I stabbed you in the side. All these years I blamed Mama for your wrongdoings and she didn't deserve that type of treatment. I just wanted to be a good daughter, and she could never understand that. Neither could I. The first time you molested me, I thought it was normal. Faith said there would be happy days after the storm, and I could never believe her because you would always go on a spree and take advantage of me every Sunday while Mama was at church. Every time she invited me to go with her, I always said no because I felt like you needed me, and I knew that God wouldn't let a dirty sinner into his sanctuary. You made me feel dirty, and developing the habit of taking five showers a day could never cleanse my soul the way God could. So now, I never miss church on Sundays. I am face-to-face with my Savior at the altar on every single Sabbath day, begging him for forgiveness and hoping that someday you will have the courage to show up and kneel down next to me to ask Him for forgiveness, too. I don't know how you've lived your life since you left me and Mama. I just hope you have been a good man, because no one else deserves to go through what you put me through. I can't forget the feeling of your scruffy beard when you forced your kisses on me, with alcohol-soaked breath and cigarette stains on your teeth or the way your tongue slipped into my mouth when you were intoxicated and acting senile. I'll never forget how you would take a piss in the bathroom and leave the door wide open for me to see. Mama was so blind to the fact that I was covered in your semen more than I was covered in shampoo or soap suds. You are the reason why I hate it when God makes it rain. Still, I forgive you, because if I don't, my real Father won't find it in his heart to forgive me, and I would like to be forgiven for every sin I have committed. I will no longer blame you. I take full responsibility for my actions and I pray that you will soon offer me an answer for why you did what you did. If not, I will still find a way to live, even if I never find my way out of this scavenger hunt.

Please write back, Your Baby Girl

Chapter 36:
Sobs of Sorrow

Mr. Henderson, Dr. Sebastian has decided that it is safe for you to visit with your wife now. It will be a supervised visit, but you will be able to interact with her as normal. The nurse has removed the shackles, but please try not to upset her."

"I'll try my best. Thank you."

"Sheila?"

"Carl?"

"Hey, baby. I missed you."

"I missed you too, Carl. Are you here to take me home?"

"No, Sheila. Not yet."

"When will I be able to go home? I am not safe here."

"As soon as they are able to find out what's wrong with you."

"How many times do I have to tell you and everybody else that there is nothing wrong with me? I am perfectly fine. See." Sheila kissed Carl before he had a chance to say what he was about to say, but he didn't kiss her back.

"Sheila, please don't do that."

"Don't do what?"

"Try to seduce me like you always do, so that I'll forget about the problems we have."

"The only problem we have is the fact that you are always resisting me."

"I am not resisting you, Sheila."

"Yes you are, Carl. You always push me away when I get sick and then you hit me!"

"Sheila, I only want what's best for you."

"Prove it then! Take me home."

"I wish I could."

"Your wish has always been my command. Why won't you let me love you? Do you hate me, Carl?"

"No, I don't hate you, Sheila. I just wish we could reverse time and possibly become the reciprocal of a bad memory that produces a better solution."

"Well, why do you treat me the way you do? Even when I try to silence them from speaking about me."

"I don't know, Sheila."

"That's right. You let your fists do the talking for you."

"The first time was a mistake."

"What about every single time after?"

"I admit that it became a sick habit, Sheila. I just wanted you to be still."

"No. You wanted Sunni days all four seasons!"

"Sheila, please calm down."

"I am as calm as I can be under these conditions. Carl, I just want you to take me home. Please."

"Sheila, I can't."

"You really have grown accustomed to telling me *No*."

"I'm sorry, Sheila, but the doctor says you have to stay here for six weeks."

"Six weeks? I cannot last even six more days in here without you, Carl. Please take me home."

"Sheila, that's the problem. You have to learn how to stand without me."

"Why? Are you leaving me, Carl? Please don't leave me. I'll change. I promise."

"No, Sheila, I am not leaving you. I just want you to get better."

Carl was crying again, and this time he couldn't hide it. Sheila grabbed his hand and locked her fingers into his. He looked at her and smiled, but the tears would not stop flowing, and Sheila began to cry, too.

"How did we get here, Carl?"

"I don't know, Sheila, but I'm sorry. I'm so sorry for hurting you."

"Don't worry about it, Carl. Take me home and I'll forgive you." Sheila wanted to hold him forever, but the guard grabbed her by the arm and made her let go.

"Mr. Henderson, it is time for you to leave now."

"Just a few more seconds, please. I need more time with my wife."

"I'm sorry, Mr. Henderson. Your time is up."

Carl was quickly taken away. Sheila didn't know for sure if she would ever get to see him again. *Who am I to turn to now? I can't even depend on my own husband to protect me.* She knew that her time was running out.

Chapter 37:
Do You See What I See?

I saw it coming, but I was blinded by the urge to be loved. I wanted Carl to want me as much as I wanted him, but instead he made me suffer. There was no escaping his wrath, so I figured it was best for me to just stay. I thought I could handle it. I knew that someday he would realize he was wrong for hurting me, and that change would soon come. He was destined to ask me for forgiveness. Genuine forgiveness, that wouldn't be followed by another beating. I prepared myself for it. I would smile and then cry, possibly find the strength to say, "Go to hell." But I want Carl to be happy, even if he doesn't end up with me.

I've always felt most comfortable in intimate settings. It just doesn't feel right when you're in those settings alone, with no one who even seems to find you valuable enough to help you search for a real ounce of peace. Aren't our souls designed to attach to a perfect match? I must not fit anyone's ideal scenario for love. I wish I could create scenes with someone who wants to deeply understand me while ignoring my emotional and physical scars. Band-Aids couldn't always help me heal, but I wore them anyway. I have found ways to disappoint everyone, even by accident. If I sketch the letter *S* enough times on the surface, maybe they can figure out the clues to my story. I just may not be stable when they do. Carl is long gone. He will probably never come back to visit me, and that's understandable. I want him to start a new life with someone new — someone who won't make him suffer as much as I have.

I knew it was too much for him to put up with me all these years. I came with a lot of baggage. He tried his best though. I couldn't ask for much more. I just want people to know that he did all that he could to try and save me. He only beat me in private because he wanted me to be Sunni all the time. But I could never give him a definite answer for when she was coming back. He truly does love me. I don't think he was intentionally bruising my alter ego out of spite. He was literally trying to knock some sense into me, but I was always too far gone.

Wet dreams are no sweat. I'll always miss him, and the way he used to sex me like crazy before I started acting like I had no mind of my own. I knew he didn't want me to compare him to Daddy, but it was inevitable. Out of all the synonyms in the dictionary, I couldn't think of one that separated them. Carl was my sailor and Daddy was always the conductor of my ship. Whether I snored or snoozed to bask in the glory of our time together, the seconds always solidified my expectations. They were both a significant part of my life, offering substantial evidence for the power of love. Even if I tried to divide the sectionals to create more room for a sequence of memorable events, I would not have much space left for details. I spent every semester of my life synchronizing my ideas, and never even considered composing a book, but writing was always my way out. It was a way for me to ignore the syllables and focus on the miniscule units of language that others weren't skilled enough to envision. Writing is the only form of therapy I've ever needed. I'm just creatively insane, and they are trying to diagnose me as a menace to society.

I would never harm anyone who allows me to share my gift, with no holds barred and no chains to strap me down. Words are like water. They drip into my spirit and quench my thirst. Whenever I'm feeling dehydrated, I just pick up my pen and new subjects flow like liquids, across natural springs of Zephyrhill Mountains, sparkling over the sand. It's been a while since I've had a real vacation. Maybe I should run away again.

Chapter 38:
A Sinner's Prayer

I guess my thoughts got lost in the shuffle of Carl's anger. He would always hit me right when I was about to recall the scenes of yesterday. Today, I feel so sad, and I'm tired of feeling sad. If he would have listened to me he would have understood me a lot better, but he liked to silence me just like them. I don't even know what I did wrong. I always tried my best to soothe him with my undying love, but it seemed as if he wanted me to die instead.

What day is it? It can't be Sunday because Sunni isn't here. I miss her. I haven't seen her since I introduced her to Brenda and Faith. She was supposed to meet me here. I hope she doesn't stand me up. I need her more than anything else I've ever needed in my whole entire life. Sunni gets me. And I get her. The world is just going to have to understand that. Brenda and Faith will move on and forget about me. I've chosen to be with the woman I love and no one can stop it.

Sunni is that you? I can't see in the dark. Say something ... *Sunni? Sunni!* I guess she's gone. She must not love me anymore. I've done too much to push her away. She doesn't fully understand our struggle. How could she be so selfish? She's just like Carl ... only cares about herself and what she wants. What about me? Don't I deserve someone who values me enough to stick around? Am I really that sick? *Sunni, can you hear me?* She must really be standing her ground. I said I was sorry for trying to kill her so many times. Are my apologies not sacred enough for her to accept? I at least thought they were delivered with enough substance to last longer than seven seconds. When I say my prayers I always ask God to keep her safe. I wonder if she does the same for me. I mean, can't she find it in her heart to forgive me after seven seconds of apologies? I don't have enough strength to scream out an eighth. I was only trying to make things better for Carl so that he wouldn't be forced to choose between us. Deep down inside I knew that he would choose Sunni, but I just couldn't let her win. Now my heart is in shambles and this skit is lasting way too long. *Are you playing games with me Sunni? Sunni! Answer me please! I need you to say something.*

"Sheila who are you talking to?"

"Sunni."

"Sunni who? You can't keep creating these imaginary worlds and people if you want me to believe that you're making progress."

"They're not imaginary. They're real."

"What makes you think so?"

"I can feel it. I know it. Don't make me think I'm crazy, Doc."

"Sheila, I am trying to help you."

"No, you're not. You're trying to ruin me like everybody else."

"That's not true."

"Yes, it is. Since day one you have been refuting my story and treating me like a deranged madwoman!"

"Sheila, lower your voice please."

"No! I can speak as loudly as I want. You obviously haven't been hearing me when I speak the truth in monotone."

Sunni, come back! I still love you! Sunni, I can't breathe without you. Sunni, I miss your sunshine. Sunni, show me where you are. I must be able to savor your special traits; your ability to speak and then listen. The way you smile at me when I feel like no one even sees me. Sunni, don't you know you're all I've got? Sunni, are you with God? If so, Sunni, tell Him I'm coming to meet Him soon because I can't handle being in solitary confinement for six weeks.

Sunni, can you feel this shower of tears streaming down my face? I'm sailing now. Are you sinking with me? Sunni? Sunni! We've only got six seconds left! I need you to come back to tell them the truth! Sunni please tell me you love me before I go!

Chapter 39:
Sweet Dreams

*M*y suitor has suited me with his aggressive nature. He likes to control me sexually, yet he says I'm the control freak. I love his sense of exploration, the way he searches for spots that have not been touched in centuries, a simile of pleasure ... like strawberries and whipped cream, without the leaves. I want my juices to flow with the stream of his stroke. I hope he can swim...

Sex came before an "I love you" in the early morning of December seventeenth, but I wasn't as devastated as I should have been. He politely told me to remove his pants, and began to stroke me gently for about seven minutes, until I made him stop. It was not like me to let a man take control with sensual offerings before addressing me with a title, nor was I familiar with this feeling. I felt careless and spontaneous at the same time ... free in a sense. Like I was the only thing that mattered to him in those seconds of us connecting sexually for the first time. Of course I cried, but he soaked up my tears with a sorry of regret, and caressed me so sweetly, as if he wanted to reverse the short moment of pleasure we had just shared. Before reaching the height of my emotional climax, I could not breathe. He was just the length I imagined and a perfect fit to my secluded area of privacy. He searched my inner area with ease. In and out, entering and exiting with extreme care. We made music together — a beautiful song that I don't want to be over until the fat lady comes to sweep us away with her final tune. He noticed the uncertainty in my facial expressions and gestures and asked how he could make it right. I told him that I wanted to pray, so he sincerely asked God to forgive us for the sin we committed, and then held me tightly after the *amen* and told me that he will always protect me.

The tears disappeared and I resumed sleep smiling, because after looking into his eyes and experiencing all he has to give, it was confirmed that the one had finally found me. I just hoped he would understand. He was the first man I allowed myself to be with after my initial healing, and I wanted to love him forever.

I never thought that I would fall out of love with Carl, but Sunni gave me more. So much more. Where is she?

Chapter 40:
Out of Sight, Out of Mind

Every time I looked at the clock, it just so happened to be 9:11. I don't know what God was trying to tell me, but it must have been urgent. How was I supposed to answer the ringing with no phone in sight and no operator available to screen my calls? I've said all I need to say anyway. There's not much more I can muster up from these scrambled thoughts of mine. Who would believe that I would ever run out of words? I'm a writer. Vivid snapshots are automatic, but I usually close my eyes before the flash. I tend to panic in the middle of an emergency. I don't know if I should call for help or try to save everyone and everything myself. I am not that strong. They keep telling me to be, but I don't know how.

I prayed and waited ... waited and prayed. OK, so what now? Where's your so-called God, Faith? I'm tired of looking like a fool talking to this imaginary person who is supposed to miraculously save me from this hell I'm in. How could I be so stupid? There is no real God! If there was, then why does He make me suffer like this? And why doesn't He ever show up when I really need Him?

Liltera R. Williams

Brenda

Liltera R. Williams

Chapter 41:
No Ordinary Love Like Sade

"Well, well, well … if it isn't Miss Stop-n-Go."

"Officer Handsome?"

"I would say it's nice to see you again if it wasn't under the same circumstances. You are one hard woman to catch."

"I only stop when I'm forced to. I'm just always in a hurry."

"This isn't the same car you were in last time."

"I know. It's my husband's. My car is on life support."

"Husband?"

"That's neither here nor there. Are you going to handcuff me and lock me up this time?"

"It would be my pleasure, as long as you're willing to cooperate."

"I always do exactly as I'm told."

"I'll beg to differ."

"Well I don't like men who beg."

"License and registration, please, ma'am."

"I thought I told you to call me Brenda during our last encounter."

"I don't like addressing women by their first name."

"What else don't you like?"

"Being stuck on the side of the road with serial offenders."

"Who, me?"

"Yes, you, ma'am."

"I am not a serial offender. I just have a problem with being in the wrong place at the wrong time."

"So, I take it you don't believe in fate?"

"Absolutely not. I believe that everything happens for a reason and fate has nothing to do with it."

"Interesting."

"There are more interesting things about me. Are you brave enough to find out?"

"Brave? I'm a police officer. We are trained to be brave."

"What's your sign?"

"Excuse me?"

"I asked you what's your sign? Or are you too strict to believe in astrology?"

"Sagittarius."

"Figures."

"How so?"

"You are obsessed with following rules."

"What about you?"

"What do you want to know about me?"

"What's your sign and why do you enjoy breaking the rules?"

"I am a Capricorn. I enjoy breaking all the rules because they are set in place for us to do so. Only the strong survive."

"I see."

"Are you ever going to tell me your real name, Officer Handsome?"

"Shawn."

"Shawn what?"

"Shawn Smith."

"Nice to meet you, Officer Shawn Smith."

He didn't even have to say much. Our magnetic attraction spoke volumes. He was affectionate, sensitive, charming, open, and so willing to reveal everything about himself, when all I really wanted to do was have sex. He tried to connect with me on an emotional level, and I thought I wasn't ready to give myself away to anyone other than Carl. The only thing that stumped me about him was his habit of repeating every single thing I said, like he was trying to spy on my brain and snoop for more revelations. He wouldn't dare try to steal me away from my husband, though. As long as he obeyed my rules, I was satisfied. He tried to be slick a couple of times, but when he did, I reminded him that I would slice him where it hurts the most. He was my Saturday night splurge … the only other man I fucked when I was sober. I allowed him to see me fully naked and we even kissed in the mornings. He loved taking me shopping, and instead of meeting me at a hotel, he let me enter his studio apartment. He said I was the only woman who was worthy of sleeping in. Breakfast in bed was a starter snack. He even liked to spoon. When I told him I couldn't see him anymore, he got angry, but he calmed down quickly. He understood my dilemma. I had a man waiting at home for me — my husband, Carl. And Shawn was just a sideline player who got to experience me when I wasn't myself at all. My need to be away from the chaos reminded me of Mama. I assume that's why she worked so much, except my line of work was different. In essence, our strategy was the same. She just didn't have to trade places with anyone.

Hell hath no fury like a woman scorned. Mama's misery became a sculpture for life's lessons, and I was never too studious to learn something new. The sequential elements of her desire to withdraw from Daddy's limited accounts of affection left her bankrupt and broken. I was sprinting toward a path that I hoped would lead to change, longing for someone to offer a penny for my thoughts because they weighed me down. Through quarter centuries of shakes and bruises, Mama was never worth more than a dime, and I was Daddy's nickel. He deposited and cashed me out before I was able to gain any interest. Negative balances went unnoticed and no one ever threatened him with a penalty, although he was careless when it came to handling important money.

Liltera R. Williams

Faith

Liltera R. Williams

Chapter 42:
Let the Church Say Amen

Praise the Lord. Hallelujah and all that jazz. I can't stand these fake Christians. I'm only here because Faith invited me. I'm not expecting God to even acknowledge my presence. I'd rather be at home sipping on some ice cold Grey Goose with a lemon. I wonder what De'Angelo is doing.

Good morning, Saints.

Oh, now here comes the preacher getting ready to tell us that we're all going to hell if we don't start acting right. Definitely sipping on some Grey Goose right after the clock strikes twelve. That's if we even get dismissed on time.

Let us pray. Dear Heavenly Father, we thank you for bringing us all here today with clear minds and sanctified spirits ready to absorb your Word. Allow us to be graciously hypnotized by your power, Lord.

Graciously hypnotized?

Let us all gain an understanding of the message you have placed inside my heart this day in time. We thank you for your blessings, for your unselfish nature to forgive us for our sins, and for giving us one more day to get it right under your guidance. In Jesus name. Amen."

Well, at least that was shorter than the last time I visited, and two years ago he was still asking God for the same thing. God is either deaf, blind or both, because He obviously can't see or hear what's going on down under. Even Christians are sinking, so why should I make an attempt to swim? And Faith was just sitting there clinging to her Bible ... holding on for dear life, expecting a Word that runs past the periods and commas meant for pause.

If God wants me to stop what I'm doing, He better give me a good reason why I should, because I ain't with this phony shit.

"Brenda, snap out of it!"

I guess I really am allergic to the Holy Ghost. Must have been daydreaming the whole time.

"Is it time to go yet?"

"How rude can you be, Brenda? God is not pleased."

"Well, it's a good thing I'm not exactly trying to please Him, isn't it?"

"You're going to hell."

"See you there. Where's my purse?"

I hate when she gets like this — upset because I won't bow down to her God. If I could see Him, it would probably be much easier to practice that impossible action she's named after. Let me check my phone.

There's only one way to be sure that God is real. Why can't Brenda see it? She's so blinded by what she wants and needs that God can't even rescue her from danger at her own hands. I wish she would stop wasting my time with her false accusations of hope. God is not a toy. She's been spending way too much time in this fictitious world and I'm losing my advantage. And I don't know how I'm supposed to persuade Sheila to hold on just a little while longer when she thinks she has no reason to live. If Sheila can't get through to Carl so that he understands how much she needs him to help her, I know I can't. He has always ignored me. So I won't even try to approach him with my pleas for him to intervene. Sheila thinks he's her savior anyway and that's the problem. She worships the wrong God. If she would just stop for a second to realize the difference between worldly and spiritually driven love, then she would have no problem speeding through her recovery.

Dear God,

Where are you? Sheila needs you. Brenda needs you. I need you. Help me get through to them. Sheila seems to be getting the point, but Brenda keeps sashaying around her with those pessimistic thoughts. I need some assistance down here. I know that I have an assignment to complete and I'm supposed to bring my sistas together, but this is getting harder and harder as each day goes on. Brenda is a tough soul to repair. She needs Holy sutures to patch up those slashes of insurmountable hurt. God show me what to do. Allow me to get my sistas to understand that we are one. In the name of the Father, the Son and the Holy Ghost.

"Not this again. Give it up, Faith. The Holy Ghost isn't real. Neither is God."

"Watch it, Brenda! I cannot continue to associate with nonbelievers."

"Whatever. I didn't need you back then and I don't need you now."

"I'll continue to pray for you, Brenda."

"Please spare me. Your prayers don't do anything but make things worse. Save your hopeless plea bargains. I'm sure your mighty God has better things to do with His time. Get real, Faith."

"I'm as real as it gets, Brenda."

"I know what's real, Faith, and you are far from it."

"Call Him!"

"Call who?"

"Jesus!"

"Are you serious right now?"

"Yes, I am serious, Brenda. It's time for you to wake up!"

"I am awake. What has Sheila been telling you?"

"I don't have to talk to Sheila to find out what's going on. God knows all and sees all and He talks to me."

"Now I know you've lost it.

"I may have lost it, but at least I know I'm saved."

"Saved from what exactly, Faith?"

"Whatever it is that is attacking you, Brenda. I'm only trying to help."

"You can't help me, Faith. No one can."

"That's not true. Open up your heart and let me. Sheila wants to help, too."

"Sheila doesn't care about me or you. Don't let her fool you. All she cares about is Carl. She left me stranded years ago and never cared enough to look back."

Sheila

Liltera R. Williams

Chapter 43:
Some Seeds Can Grow Without Water

Dear Mama,

I forgive you. That's all you really need to know. What's done in the dark will eventually come to the light and I have been seeking the truth for so long. I don't know what it was that caused me to turn out this way, but I'm pretty sure it started with Daddy. The doctors said my condition was primarily caused by some sort of traumatic event. I can't even select an option for which one was most severe. Daddy's sexual abuse stemmed your verbal abuse, and Carl's physical abuse was not an effective solution. It's too late to keep shifting the blame.

When you throw Hail Mary passes they are free to be intercepted, and I know the differences between football and soccer. Kicking balls around is what got me here in the first place—mentally unstable with an STD. I got even sicker from the medication, so there is no point in scribbling down a routine schedule. Nothing is easy for me to remember anymore. My hard drive has become too full for the capabilities of a Sanyo or Samsung device. Flashbacks are all I can seem to recall. But Mama, I just want you to know that it was not your fault. I let Daddy continue to stick me with his sharp edge. I was just never able to get you to see the scars. You were always too busy for me when I needed you. I know that Daddy wasn't the best husband, but he needed you, too. I wish I didn't have to fill in your role. I wanted to just keep telling him *no*. But I was afraid that he wouldn't love me. I couldn't be left high and dry without love from anyone.

I'm still learning how to love myself, but I'm getting there. My sistas have helped me a lot. Even though you never took the time to really get to know them, they appreciated you for bringing me into the world. You said it would do me no good to carry on my connection to them and I tried to tell them goodbye so many times. I just couldn't let Brenda and Faith go. I bet you would love Sunni. She's always so positive. She helps me deal with the bad days. I've been missing her lately, though. I miss you, too, Mama. I haven't heard back from you since the last time we talked. I hope the doctors were able to keep your cancer under control. Daddy never found me. I wouldn't know what to say to him if I ever saw him again anyway. I assume it would be an awkward reunion, with him apologizing over and over again. I really did think he was dead. I wrote him a letter, too. I told him that I forgive him. I have to forgive you both if I want to move forward and be healthy. That's what Dr. Sebastian keeps telling me. Forgiveness is a command that God gives. Faith told me that. She and Dr. Sebastian seem to be on the same page.

I also read somewhere that strong women wear their pain like stilettos. I'm hurting, but you can still see my beauty. I guess I'm strong. I've been strong enough to make it this far. Maybe I'm not ready to die. If I never get to see you again, Mama, I hope you will find some happiness before God calls you home. And maybe ... just maybe ... this letter will offer you some peace.

Brenda

Chapter 44:
Sight-Seeing

What the hell is wrong with me? Why do I keep having this same nightmare?

Brenda didn't think she would ever forget what happened to her. Every time she reached for an inch of happiness, she would always flash back to the horrible moment ... lying dormant on the floor of her bedroom, almost drowning in a pool of tears, and the sound of her father's scream would never be erased from her memory. She would be haunted forever by that day. All she ever wanted to do was forget it ever happened and forget he ever existed.

"Why are you so quiet all of a sudden, Sheila? You had plenty to say about Carl earlier." I know you love him more than you love me."

"Now is not the time, Brenda."

"Well, when is the time to tell you how selfish you've been?"

"Selfish?"

"Yes, selfish!"

"I am not the selfish one, Brenda. You are. And Faith can back me up on that."

"Don't try to bring Faith into this. All you care about is Carl."

"He's my husband! Why are you so jealous of my relationship with him? I make time for you when I can."

"That is the biggest lie I've been spanked with all day. Tell me something new."   "You need help, Brenda. Have a drink and soak yourself in your own sorrow. I'm tired of you sabotaging my sanity."

"Sheila, you just don't realize that the choice is yours. It always has been."

"What choice are you talking about?"

"The choice to leave!"

"And go where? Do what?"

"Be happy."

"There's no such thing as happy."

"See, there's the problem."

"What problem?"

"I can't be happy without you. And neither can Faith. You've been shutting us out for so long … living in your own little world … writing all day in your notebooks … forgetting about who was there for you from the very beginning."

"I know who to thank, Brenda."

"I'm not asking for a thank you."

"Well, what do you want from me?"

"I want happiness … for you, for me, for us, Sheila. Aren't you tired of all of this?"

"The only thing that I'm tired of is the fact that you keep overwhelming me with your own personal needs. What about me, Brenda? What about what I need?"

"We all need the same thing, Sheila, but you're too set in your ways to realize it. At least I'm finally acknowledging the issue."

"My issues have been resolved. When you get to happy, please let me know how and where to find it."

"Is that how things will end?"

"Things ended between us a long time ago. Move on! I have."

"No, you haven't, Sheila. You've been hiding just like me. It's time for us both to step up to the plate and reveal our secret."

"I don't have any secret to reveal. You think life is a game, Brenda. Do you ever stop to wonder why you're the only one playing?"

"What the hell does that mean?"

"It means it's time for you to call a timeout on your concern and forfeit your right to express an opinion about my life. I know what I'm doing."

"Well, why are you doing it? Do you aim to torture me on purpose?"

"No, I aim to stay as far away from you as possible. Stop following me!"

I wonder what season it is. I'm left here imagining what stays current on the outside. My superstar status has disappeared. I'm no longer important to the various suspects who think I've lost my mind. I just had a hard time focusing because God never clearly told me which station to pay attention to. The channels have so much static now, and my ears are sore. I wish I could co-wash myself in someone

236

else's concern and let them soothe me, or swallow sips of a sweet white wine. This is too stressful for me to deal with all by myself. I still need something that starts with an *S* ... a strong strategy for escaping.

Liltera R. Williams

Faith

Liltera R. Williams

Chapter 45:
Still Seeing Things

"Sheila, you have serious issues and wishing you were white won't make them disappear."

"How do you know that? White people have it easy. I've always had it hard."

"Things are not hard because you're black; they're hard because you're stubborn."

"I am not stubborn, Faith."

"Yes, you are. One day you will realize how much you've gotten in your own way over the years. I just hope it's not too late."

"Who are you to judge? Just because you're saved, it doesn't mean that you are better than me. We all have our problems. You can't fool me, Faith. There isn't that much change in the world. Nobody's perfect. So, what's your secret?"

"I don't keep secrets. There's nothing that any of us can hide from God."

"Well, if God knows everything that I've done wrong, what's the point of confessing?"

"It shows Him that you are ready to acknowledge your sins and move forward."

"Well, I'm not ready."

"When will you be ready, Sheila?"

"Shouldn't God know?"

"Yes, but it's up to you to decide if you want it."

"Want what?"

"The blessing."

"Can't you just share yours? I don't have time to bow down for whatever it is that God is trying to offer me."

"Sheila, hell is real and you are headed straight there if you don't wake up."

"I don't need to hear a sermon, Faith, especially when we both know that your past isn't so lovely."

"This isn't about me. This is about you, Sheila. Don't you dare try to flip the guilt script. I will continue to pray that God heals you and delivers you from your past."

"No need."

You're your own worst enemy, Sheila. Let me help you, Sheila. Listen to me, Sheila. Pray, Sheila. Give it to God, Sheila. I'm so sick of Faith and her need to control me. She is not my mother and she can't tell me what to do.

"He beat you to a pulp, and you still went back. Don't call me when you're on your death bed!"

That's the last thing Brenda said to me. I'm not going to call her now that I'm where she predicted I would end up. She wouldn't rescue me anyway. I really need Sunni, but I don't know if she's willing to come back after that last argument we had.

"Don't talk to me that way, Sheila. You and I both know that I don't belong here."

"I'm sorry, Sunni."

"Are you really? I will not allow you to keep treating me this way. I've bent over backwards to do everything that you wanted. I seduced Carl for you and then you got mad when he fell in love with me. I left you alone when you needed your space. You don't know what it is that you truly want, Sheila, and I can't decide for you. You put me in the middle and then you turned on me when things didn't work out as planned. What else could you possible want from me?"

"I want you to forgive me, Sunni. Please."

"Forgive you? Now you want forgiveness?"

"Yes."

"Why should I forgive you, Sheila?"

"Because I love you."

Faith

Liltera R. Williams

Chapter 46:
So I Guess This Is Goodbye

"Hey, Faith. How is Sheila doing?"

"Save it! Don't act like you care now, Brenda. Where were you when she was calling? I'm sure she would have loved to hear your voice. Now it might be too late to even say sorry. Don't you know how much she valued you? You were her favorite friend before she started holding those psychotic conversations in her head. I tried praying for her, but my prayers weren't enough. She needed both of our support. But you were too selfish to even show up when she needed you the most. How could you abandon her, Brenda?"

"Faith, please stop! What do you want me to say? I had my own problems to deal with. I didn't have the strength to help someone else. You said God would be there on time, Faith. That was a lie! He didn't show up for me or for her. I'm so used to broken promises that I can't even blame Him. I blame you, Faith! You made us believe in something and someone who doesn't even exist. Now that's what I call a sin. Everything else is called surviving, and that's what I've always done, no matter where I was or who I was sleeping with. You're the one who kept feeding us stale soup while you were enjoying your last supper with the saints. How's the Pastor doing, by the way? He must really be in shackles now, begging God for forgiveness on your behalf. And what about you? Is God going to automatically forgive you because you're saved and sanctified? Look in the mirror, Faith. Because the only Satan I've ever seen is you. So save that sappy shit for the hypocrites like you who need it. But for the record, I'm sorry. Tell Sheila that I'll see her on the other side where it was always Sunni. Selah, my dearly beloved sista. I'm off to see if God is as real as you say He is."

Brenda swiftly shed her clothing and surrendered to the Lord. "OK, my sweet Savior, the clock has stopped and I hear the song. Tonight, I will not lie down to suffer. Naked I came into this world and naked I shall return unto you. I surrender to the cross. I'm tired of running."

Take me to the King...

Sheila sang the song with sour tears in her eyes, but there was one more thing she needed to do so that God would not stamp her as one that was insane. She offered Him herself as a salutation, hoping that He would understand her motive.

I have not forgotten you, Sheila.

God had spoken, but Sheila was already covered in silence. The doors of Heaven slowly opened and Sheila entered. *God, I heard you talking to me! I am here to receive the message.*

Do you have enough strength to believe that God will eventually show up? Can He trust you to trust Him? He always appears suddenly and suddenly often comes soon. Keep the faith. Sunni days are not too far away.

Sheila gave way to her new guise, but she wasn't expecting to receive any more bad news.

Sheila

Liltera R. Williams

Chapter 47:
Double Suicide

"Mrs. Henderson, we have a letter for you."
"Who is it from?"
"Your husband."
"Carl?"

fter receiving the full rundown on Sheila's condition, Carl snuck out of the hospital against doctor's orders. He Aaccepted the blame for Sheila's current state and there was nothing else that he could do to fix it. Carl wanted to eliminate himself so that Sheila would no longer be forced to suffer at his hands. He was sorry and he meant it, but somehow, over the years he lost control of himself. Loving Sheila wasn't easy, but Carl thought he had things covered. When Sheila revealed excerpts from her past one by one, Carl tried his best to deal with it. It got to be too much and Carl knew that he had to do something about it so that he would stop hurting Sheila. At this point, he just didn't know how to love her sane.

Sheila,

I know this apology may be seconds too late, but I just want to be sure you know how much I've always loved you. You were my songbook before I was even blessed with the lyrics to fill it up. I have spent the past seven years of my life loving you and I couldn't ask God for a more spectacular way of showing me that I was worthy enough to be responsible for someone so beautiful. However, I have failed Him. My purpose was to save you, and I couldn't. Instead, I damaged you more with my selfish need to be pleased by you only when you were calm. I wish I could fall out of love with Sunni to bring Sheila back. But she stole my heart the moment she expressed her sincerest reasons for wanting and needing me. You were never that open with me, Sheila. I so desperately needed you to show me a sign that you were capable of changing. It became too difficult for me to accept the fact that my spouse was not the woman whom I anticipated her to be. When the doctors told me that you had Schizophrenia, I thought they were the ones who were insane. How could you be four people at once? That was the most shocking news I could ever receive. I was committing adultery with a supernatural force of nature, and figured God must have wanted to punish me. I took it out on you. I'm so sorry, Sheila. I don't know what else to say, so I'm saving you from myself to guarantee that I will never strike you again. I'll personally ask God to cover you because He always knows what's best. I hope you will sleep peacefully tonight. Maybe I'll see you on the other side someday. Things were bright and Sunni on your end, even when the sun was setting. I will always love you, Sheila, even after 'til death do us part.

P.S. Never Give Up Hope,
Carl

Sirens could be heard just seconds after Carl's severe exit. The gun shot was so loud that the neighbors were immediately stricken by the sound. The cops were on their way to deliver Carl the news about Sheila's latest suicide attempt, but her Superman was already prepared to save her.

"No, Carl! No!"
"Mrs. Henderson, we're so sorry."

With snot at the cusp of my upper lip, I couldn't help but let the tears win. A widow's peak never stretches far enough for you to be able to identify the exact date or time that your spouse will demand a separation. Carl gave me no warnings and no signs that he was at his wit's end, other than pieces of scraps from his fists. Subways never lead to common ground, and I obviously was never good at following directions. Is this how it ends, God? After all my Sunday meetings with Faith, and her telling me that things would eventually get better? I don't want better if this is it. Give me normal. That's all I've ever asked you for — a normal life with people who genuinely love and care about me. Am I not worth it, God? Why did you take my husband away from me? You know he's the only one who was capable of dealing with my mess. I guess I should have thrown the trash out when it was stinking up my surroundings instead of carrying it around with me for too long. Why, God? You're never able to tell me why. The need to know why is my curse and my gift, and I get the feeling that I'll be returning a few things when you're through with me. I am not strong enough to handle this alone. You know that. Please stop making me suffer. I've done all that I can to prove to you that I am willing to get help. I'm here — right here waiting for you to take me away from this hell on earth. I have no more reasons for breathing. My air is gone and I am still suffocating after all these years of abuse, neglect, and disappointment. I have sinned and I am sorry. How many times will you require me to say it? I have fallen short of your glory on numerous occasions. The seasons still change, so I know there must be a treasure for me at the end of the rainbow. This is no soliloquy, God. I am speaking directly to you ... no microphones, no stages and no audience to give me applause at the end. Show me something good for once, because it hurts so badly.

Liltera R. Williams

Brenda

Liltera R. Williams

Chapter 48:
Summing It All Up

T hings had unfolded too quickly for Brenda to fully comprehend. Dr. Sebastian needed to make sure that she was making real progress … if she was finally able to accept who she really was. All of the stories she had told Dr. Sebastian were not making complete sense. Brenda's thoughts were all over the place. It was clear that she was a schizophrenic, but identifying her individual personalities was not a common act. Why did she change her name to Sheila? Was Faith a real person? And exactly who was Sunni? It took Dr. Sebastian years to figure Brenda out. She had been counseling her on the abuse from her father, but was not informed about these other symptoms until now. How did she miss this? Brenda did a great job of hiding her various sides, but Dr. Sebastian had never been fooled to this degree. She was more confused than ever and had yet to be duped by any patient. She tried to get to the bottom of it and hoped Brenda would be able to cooperate.

"Are you awake?"

"Yes, I am."

"I think we need to recap. I'm not quite sure if you have told me the entire truth about your life outside of therapy. Our once-a-week sessions didn't allow me to gain full insight into all that you have experienced and I don't have anyone else's word to lean on but yours. Do you think you're well enough to tell me the truth?"

"I have been telling you the truth."

"Well, let's start over. Are you up for it?"

"I guess so."

"What's your name?"

"Brenda."

"When were you born?"

"November 23, 1976."

"Husband? Kids?"

"I had a husband, but he's dead now. So is my daughter, Savannah."

"Can you recall what happened to them?"

"Carl killed himself because I drove him crazy and Savannah died after our car accident."

"I'm sorry for your family loss. Do you know where you are?"

"Yes."

"Can you tell me?"

"A sanitarium."

"How did you end up here?"

"I tried to kill myself again."

"Why?"

"I don't know. It's the only way for me to escape the noise."

"What noise?"

"The conversations."

"Conversations between who?"

"My sistas."

"Sheila and Faith?"

"Yes."

"Can you tell me who they are again?"

"Sheila is the new me. I changed my name and my appearance when I became legal. I didn't want anyone to recognize me. Faith is my angel."

"Your angel?"

"Yes, she reassured me every time I did something wrong. She spoke to God for me."

"Who is Sunni?"

"Sunni is my hero."

"How so?"

"She watched over me everywhere that I went. She kept trying to save me, but I could never make a decision between her and Carl. I wanted to be with Sunni, but she left before I could make up my mind."

"Do you know where she is?"

"No, but I hope she isn't gone for good."

"Do you remember anything about your parents?"

"Yes. I remember my mama calling to tell me that she had breast cancer and that my daddy was looking for me."

"They both came to visit when you were unconscious. We couldn't wake you."

"I guess that's a good thing. I wouldn't have known how to respond to that."

"Brenda, we've done everything that we can to restore your memory. It seems like it's only a temporary fix. Your six weeks are up, but I don't know if it's a good idea to let you go home."

"Why not?"

"You may relapse at any time and there is no one who can commit to taking care of you now that your husband is gone."

"I can take care of myself."

"I really wish you could, Brenda. I would like to believe that you have been completely healed, but there is no permanent cure for Schizophrenia."

"Schizophrenia?"

"Yes, that's what we have diagnosed you with."

"So, you're telling me that I'm crazy."

"No, not crazy. Just a little unbalanced. We need to keep monitoring your progress for a while so that we can be sure about our diagnosis."

"So, I'll never be able to have a life again?"

"I'm not saying *never*. Just not right now, Brenda. Trust me; it's for your own good. I'm going to leave and allow you to get some rest, but continue pondering about your past and I will return to ask you some more questions. I'm glad to see you're doing well."

Sunni

Chapter 49:
I Once Was Lost, but Now I'm Found

"Sunni, where's Mommy? You said she was going to meet us here. Why isn't she here yet? I miss her."

"Just be patient, Savannah. She's coming."

"Is Daddy coming, too?"

"I don't think so."

"Why not? I've been a good girl. You said if I behaved that my daddy would love me."

"I know, Savannah. I'm sorry. I can't control what he does. I am only here to look after you until your mother joins us."

"Well, when is she coming, Sunni? Are you going to leave me?"

"Savannah, calm down and be patient, please. I'm not going anywhere. I'm here to stay."

I would tell you to slap me and call me Susan, but my name is Sunni ... and I am sane. It happened on a Sunday when my soul was at stake. I can't tell you all of the specific details because I'm still recovering from the symptoms. I lost about seventy pounds, though. Carl never liked me skinny. I miss his smell. He would have loved to see me finally stepping into my season of sacrifice. The last time he snapped at me, I was too stubborn to sit still, but it was only because God kept calling my name. I was led astray into this supersized building. There were so many people there. I had to undergo a case study and they ran a bunch of tests. I even had to get stitches for the slit on my forehead. I can't remember everything, so I'll just skip to the best scene when I entered the gates of heaven! My surroundings were so serene. I could only hear my heart beating after the song finally stopped. Then, I saw the light.

It was a serendipitous discovery.

"Brenda? Brenda? Are you here?"

"Faith?"

"Yes, Brenda."

"Faith, I'm so glad it's you! I promised you that I would be strong enough and I made it out. You have no idea what it feels like to keep spinning around on an axis that hardly ever stops."

"Actually, Brenda, I do. And I'm here to tell you that God is pleased. He simply wanted you to keep believing, and though you wavered sporadically, you never lost sight of where He was taking you. There's only one stipulation now — you must repent for your sins. It is the only way that He will remove you from this asylum and allow you to live peacefully from this day forth."

"How do I do that?"

"Just be yourself and speak from your heart, Brenda."

"OK, Faith. I'll try."

Dear God,

It's been a while since I've been able to come to you in a state of normalcy, but I'm pretty sure you knew that already. I guess the first thing that I should say is I'm sorry. I know you probably hear it a lot, but this time I truly do mean it. After so many years of suffering, you still loved me enough to save me, and I thank you for that. I really don't know where I would have been if you thought I was too tainted to restore. Although I have not always depended on you or turned to you in my times of need, you were there. Thank you again. Thank you for keeping me alive when I was ready to die. Thank you for continuously blessing me with life, after the many times I've tried to take it. I know I don't deserve to live, but you've spared me for a reason. I hope that I will someday be able to live out my purpose, even though having Schizophrenia limits my options. I didn't really know how to deal with all that I've been through. I figured sex and drinking would help me forget. I almost forgot it all. And I was almost happy. Carl made me happy and I'm glad you sent him to me, God, even though my charade eventually became my curse. I'm so sorry for abusing your power, God, and for not depending on you like I should have. I just didn't know how. Every time I needed you, you took too long to show up so I just took matters into my own hands. I made a mess of it all. I tried to fix it, but it was too late. I know you may have a hard time forgiving me, but I want to make the best of whatever life I have left to live, even if I'm stuck in here forever. I think I'm finally starting to see myself for who I really am. I don't know if I will ever accept me for me, but I'm trying. I'll try harder if you let me, God. Just tell me what I need to do. I don't want to experience any more pain. I just want to be calm. I want to enjoy beautiful moments and remember what happened the next day. I know you can work miracles, God, so every day I'll be praying for one — praying for you to heal me and lead me down a greater path. This difficult test shall serve as my testimony and I will use it to prevent someone else from going down the same path. Please forgive me, Father, and save me one last time. I repent.

Amen.

From Brenda's lips to God's ears, that prayer was her final plea for restoration. She knew He heard it, but there was no immediate response. Emotions have no logic, so maybe God thought she was just speaking robotically. Brenda closed her eyes and prepared for rest. She had no idea where she would be emotionally when day came, but she knew that there was nowhere else to run.

Crazy is as crazy does, she thought. *And I'm not crazy*. It was a reminder that she hoped would stick. The last voice she heard before dozing off was Sunni's. She had returned to kick off the upcoming soiree.

"Am I my sista's keeper?" she whispered.

"Yes, Sunni. You're my ray of light."

Acknowledgments

There is no such thing as impossible. All it takes is a little faith. When I initially began to write this story, I had it all planned out. My plan was to spend a whole year working on it after graduating from college in December of 2008, but life got in the way, and I put my dream on hold ... because I had to live. However, I never stopped writing. I didn't know that it would take so much time for this story to develop. God knew what he was doing. I was just impatient. So, after building my freelance writing portfolio, forming my own writing and proofreading/editing and publishing company, being offered my first actual full-time writing job, and publishing my collection of poetry, four years later, I was finally in the "write" place and "write" position—which is what my Bishop constantly preached over the past year. I spent every day of 2012 studying and drafting in order to construct each scene. It literally came down to the last weekend of the year, and a few months past my initial deadline.

As I was living, my story was still developing and I didn't want it to end. I spent the last four days reflecting and finalizing, but the scenes were still flooding my thought process. I was finally able to wrap up the action, overlooking the beautiful beach scenery of Amelia Island. However, I was not completely satisfied. I still felt like something was missing.

Almost a whole year after my deadline of December 31, 2012. my S.I.S.T.A.S were finally at peace. *Dearly Beloved S.I.S.T.A.S* is my story. Although it is based on a fictitious concept, I believe that everyone can relate to the rawness that is displayed throughout.

I am a Child of God and I am grateful. I have the following people to thank for helping me make it through. Mom and Dad: Words cannot express how much I love you and how honored I am to have you both in my life. All my life, you both have been there ... supporting me, encouraging me, disciplining me and protecting me. I owe it all to you. Bro: I don't know what life would have been like as an only child, and I'm so glad that I never have to know. I love you and I am so proud to be your big sister. Grandma Gussie: The most selfless person I know. I love you more than words can say. Granddaddy Lilton and Grandma Vivian: I have always cherished the moments I spent with both of you, whether extended or brief. I love you both unconditionally. My deceased grandparents: Fred Curry and Deloris "Daisy" Mangram-Williams. I wish saying "I miss you" could bring you both back, but I will not question God's will. I know that you both are always watching me and I hope I have made you proud. My Aunts and Uncles: It takes a village to raise a child, and I was one of many you were responsible for looking after. I thank you all for being willing to step in to assist my parents when they needed it. My cousins: They say no one can ever come between the bonds shared between cousins. I cherish the memories that I created with all of you. To my church family at All People International, Bishop Arthur T. Jones Sr. and Pastor Sharon Jones: thank you for your ongoing prayers and support. My best friends: Rachel Winters, Riana Winters, Ashley Johnson, Alexia Larkins, Melissa Lewis and Erica Jackson. G.A.C. for life! Twon Adams: My #1 fan. Thank you for being the first and sometimes the only person to read everything I compose.

My Kickstarter backers: Kenny Smith, TL Publishing Group, Trishanda Bentley, Kenny Ford, William Alexander, Chris C.P. Gilbert, J.T. Townsend, Kotrish Wright CNP, Monya Williams, Wyan Lancelot Felton, Dr. Mervin P. Wallace, Lilton & Cassandra Williams, Al Letson, Tanaine Jenkins, J Dianne Tribble, Jerry L. Flanders Jr., Daynetha D. Singleton, Justin Lacy, Chantalle Johnson, Brittainy Simmons, Gentoria Wiley, Lesley Jones, Rachel Winters, Riana Winters, Vic Carter, Trey Ford, Carla Mechele, Belinda N. Jackson, Ruby C. Brown, JD, Miford Adams, Austin Johansen, Ryan Smith, Mary Anderson, M.A., Dedrina Reeves, Seanda Hines, LaTresa Henderson, Joshua Williams, Alicia Robinson, Reginald Louis, Tameca Porter, Danielle White, Shanae Hall, Taurean Wiggins, Karen Holm, Jasmine Greene, Kimberly Smith Tolbert, Leon Easterling, Melissa R. Allen, Tina Bossie, Thomas Josey, Melody Smith-Riggins, Courtney Carter, Angelia Menchan, Shirlyn Mobley, Phineshea Goggins, Audrey Rose, Vince Loc, Teaira Morris, April Williams, Karrie Westwood, Pamela Elliott, Melissa Lewis, Life Coach Carl Davis, Pam James, Curtis Harris, Kim Dove, Everett L. Johnson II, Louise Riofrio, Kermit Shockley Jr., Syreeta Huntley, Cynthia Butler, Antoinette Adams, JaLynne A. Santiago, Gloria Adams, LaKesha, Regina Powell, Irina Dlyankova, Denny Hilliard Jr., Chris Seville, Ron Jennings, Laymon Hicks, Altoine L. Walker, Victoria Hamilton, Xavier Gelsey, Lucinda Hightower, Chaunci

Cross, G. Double L. Productions, Darryl Reuben Hall, Jessica Jeffery, Carlos "Los2k6" Smith II, Miaya McCray, Angie Nixon, Rachel Elsea, William, Eugenia Green, Walter D. Adams, Naketa Brown, Tyrone Flagler, Tanishia Middleton, Emily Louise Skanes, Lainey Durant, Renata Hannans, Pastor R. Michael Fedd and Lady Debbie Fedd, Alexia Larkins, Charles Felton, Corey Jones.

My Editor, Sharon Denny: Thank you for being patient with me and taking the time to polish my pages!

To you, the reader: Thank you for being interested in reading my story. I hope you were able to gain something from the message that was delivered.

"If you're living without giving, your talents are null and void."

LIVE YOUR DREAM

—LRW

About the Author

Born to write in Jacksonville, Florida, Liltera R. Williams (LRW) fell in love with writing at age 12 and married it at 18. From the moment she began penciling down thoughts and ideas in her first diary, and then formally learning how to compose essays and pieces of fiction during her high school years at Samuel W. Wolfson High and college years at Florida State University, she knew that she would someday have an opportunity to share her gift with the world. Her given name was perhaps a foreshadowing of the works she would produce to establish herself in history as a Literary Legend.

Upon graduating from FSU in December of 2008 with a Bachelor's degree in English (Creative Writing), LRW began blogging, then set out to build her professional portfolio by pitching stories and completing freelance assignments for various publications. She is now well known as an International Writer, Spoken Word Poet, Bestselling Author (Amazon & UBAWA), Editor, Independent Publisher and Educator via her company, iWrite4orU, which was established in August of 2011. In addition to having over 50 articles published in Jacksonville Magazine, 904 Magazine, EU Jacksonville Newspaper, The Ponte Vedra Recorder, First Coast Register, Sister2Sister Magazine, Bazaar and Khaleejesque, her author catalog includes:

Amateur Thoughts: A Personal Collection of iWrite Poetry & LRW Quotes (Amazon Bestseller), *Dearly Beloved S.I.S.T.A.S* (UBAWA Top 100 Book of 2013 Amazon Bestseller), *Words from the Write Side of My Heart* (Amazon Bestseller), *LIVE YOUR DREAM: How to Set and Accomplish Deadline-Driven Goals* (Number One Amazon Bestseller), *PEN, PUBLISH, PROMOTE The Write Way (Detailed Guide for Aspiring Authors), LEAP: Motivation for Fearless Living (Digital Workbook)* and *Date Knight* (in progress).

After gaining a substantial amount of local support, LRW journeyed all the way from the United States to the Middle East, focused on growing internationally. She has garnered instant success overseas, from performing at Abu Dhabi's biggest monthly open mic poetry event, Rooftop Rhythms, as well as the inaugural Abu Dhabi International Poetry Festival and featuring at Word of Mouth Kuwait to hosting workshops for aspiring writers and serving as Learning Support Assistant and Poetry Club Facilitator at Kuwait English School.

In the process of developing her LIVE YOUR DREAM movement and expanding her entrepreneurial knowledge, LRW originated and trademarked a unique term to define her mission: #WriterGrind®—a strategic quest to accomplish various writing objectives while striving to conquer the demands of authorship. She specializes in helping aspiring authors discover their potential, while also offering tutoring for teens who struggle with writing and reading comprehension.

As a full-time English Teacher and the on-site College Reach-Out Program (CROP) Coordinator for Florida State University's CARE department at a high school in her hometown, Liltera is a lover of literature who believes that anything is possible with the determined mindset of Effort, Perseverance, and Faith. While adjusting to her calling in the classroom, she multi-tasked to obtain a Master of Fine Arts degree in Creative Writing from Full Sail University (October 2016). Now, she is actively pursuing her screenwriting goals and has completed two television pilot scripts.

Liltera strives to be an overall inspiration for anyone seeking to find their purpose in life, while aiming to create a legacy that will be recognized and respected for years to come.

www.ingramcontent.com/pod-product-compliance
Lightning Source LLC
Chambersburg PA
CBHW022005010726
47494CB00003B/892